NORSE MYTHOLOGY

Enchanting Tales of the Ancient World

Isaiah Covington

TABLE OF CONTENTS

INTRODUCTION

Before there was anything or anyone, before land or sea or beast, there stood *Yggdrasil*, the tree of the world. All knowledge and existence that ever was and ever will reside beneath the aged, firm bark. There was power all about it; from the apex of the tallest branches where a great eagle beat its wings without end, to the worlds beneath the very roots that brought life to the entirety of *Yggdrasil*.

There will never be a way of knowing where this mighty tree originated from, nor who may have planted the seed ages before it sprouted into such a magnificent specimen. In its resplendent branches were the scurrying chatter of *Ratatoskr*, the squirrel who carried insults and messages back and forth from the eagle in the heights to the dragon, *Nidhogg*, who slept restlessly at the base of the tree. Despite its sleep, *Nidhogg* was never alone, for it had snakes that slithered about, always alert and always gnawing at the roots of *Yggdrasil* in hopes of passing its life force to their master, the dragon.

These were not the only beasts to find safety and a home under the protection of *Yggdrasil*; four beautiful, sleek stags walked proudly about the grass where its leaves fell, grazing and soaking up the life that the tree was glad to give. *Yggdrasil*, loving the peaceful creatures that the stags proved to be, named each of the four so that they would know their home forevermore; these names were *Dainn*, *Dvalinn*, *Duneyrr*, and *Durathror*.

In the time before the cosmos and before any of creation had come into being, *Yggdrasil* was all that there was and all that had been. Yet, the tree seemed lonesome, even in its strong and mighty state. The branches, thick and sturdy, had no worlds to hold and carry, the same with the roots of the tree that desired purpose and meaning.

Unbeknownst to any of the creatures of the tree or of the fire and ice that raged about the base, something was brewing—something disparate and *large*. Deep, deep in the heart of *Yggdrasil* sparked the hint of a smile because only there was the knowledge of what was about to occur. There would be pain and strife, yes, but also joy and new beginnings—it all would come about in its own time, but for now, all the tree could do was wait with the slightest of smirks; the kind that sprung from the sides of the mouth when you knew a secret no one else did.

And what a secret it was!

CHAPTER ONE:

CREATION OF THE COSMOS

The ground was icy and thick, as it had been since it came into being, but something about this night felt odd. Cold was all that had ever existed across the entirety of *Niflheim* in a way that kept an eternal frost clinging to all that dared to either grow or trespass upon its territory. As valiant and proud as the animals that frequented the great tree of the world, *Yggdrasil,* would not dare approach *Niflheim.* Even the air surrounding the land was frigid and caused breath to turn to mist within an instant.

Such was the temperature that "ice" and "cold" barely lent a glimpse of truth to the reality of the frozen tundra. It was not dormant nor content to simply *be*; *Niflheim* was always hunting, always watching, and never stopped desiring more—more earth to freeze, more stones to shatter with the aching cold. For lack of a better word, the land of ice was alive and always craved for more.

For all the desperately dreamed notions of expanding that *Niflheim* held in its icy core, what was also watching just over the horizon yearned for all that and much more. Where *Niflheim* froze and cut off life with its icy tendrils, the land of fire did just the opposite with the same intent; *Muspelheim* wanted more, and the way to snatch it was with the way of the flame. Every inch of ground was either scorched or engulfed in the fire that seemed to lick greedily at every angle around it. Thick plumes of smoke billowed from gaping craters and smoldering piles of embers—nothing was untouched by the fiery fingers of *Muspelheim*.

Time had no place between these two realms, and as such there was no way to know how long their battle had raged for; silent as it was, the violence in its desire burned hotter than the flame and cut deeper than any freeze. It began at some point well before anyone could ever possibly remember, and the start was so small and seemingly innocuous that even the most astute seer would not have seen where it all would eventually lead.

The ice would forever claim that the flames reached beyond their boundaries first, but of course, the fire would deny that with vehement passion, insisting that the cold heart of *Niflheim* tried to overstep the territories laid forth so very long ago. However, what actually occurred mattered very little, because the spark was inevitable with the gargantuan tension that had grown between the two contrasting worlds. A catalyst for the war that was still going on, though the balance was teetering on the very edge and all that was needed for chaos to erupt was the slightest of errant breaths—the universe was simply waiting for that exhale.

Both worlds, opposite and yet raging with the same desire to expand and control, swelled and crashed against nonexistent barriers without end. In the timeless darkness, before anything was, the void was being threatened. From either side, the walls were thinning and the void itself, *Ginnungagap*, felt the walls of its territory weakening. It could feel nothing, it could not speak nor hear, yet despite a lack of senses, the hopeless glimmer of fear was hanging in the air.

Fire roared and seemed to beckon with its blaze, while from the other side of *Ginnungagap*'s breadth rose the ice and freeze that caused a mist to swirl all about the borders. There were moments when the void felt it all collapsing and there was nothing left to do but give in, yet strength returned at the last second and nothing could vanquish it. Then, without warning, sparked the beginning of the end.

From *Muspelheim* came the slow yet horrifyingly determined gait of the flames. For what seemed like an eternity, the home of fire had demanded rights to the void, while never being able to approach it to take its claim. Nothing else lived in the blazing inferno aside from the yearning; the literal, burning need to take over what lay in its path—and *Ginnungagap* was directly in the way.

Oblivious to anything outside of its attempt at conquest, the *Muspelheim* continued its barrage against the hidden barriers of *Ginnungagap*, while on the other side its eternal opposite was trying to do the same. While the land of primordial ice had no fire or flames to weaponize, the sheer sharpness of the ice itself seemed to slice right through the air around it. Wisps of mist glided through the air that was almost blue in its temperature and hue.

Where *Muspelheim* preferred the power of blunt force, the ice had a more subtle way of getting its point across. It didn't strike or slap itself against the invisible walls of *Ginnungagap*, rather it seduced the very winds that were churning from the apex of *Yggdrasil* and began to freeze the very ground that kept the ice from reaching the void. Something deeper than itself and more powerful than even the cold of *Niflheim* was calling out from the center of *Ginnungagap*.

There are points in time that are absolute and no amount of desire or hoping can alter them. These moments are very few and far between, but when they occur, it is to bring something about that was *inevitable*. It was not because *Yggdrasil* craved for something more, and it was not because of the conflict between fire and ice. The time was now, patiently waiting to come into being because the worlds were ready.

The darkness of the void, the might of *Yggdrasil*, and the bounty of fantastical creatures were not the endgame, there greater things planned. It demanded sacrifice to be born, and what great and mournful sacrifices they would be, but nothing could ever change that. Even if both flame and freeze ceased their siege of *Ginnungagap*, something else would have risen to bring forth the same outcomes. As it happened, fire and ice did not back down, nor did the void hold its walls.

That single, infinitesimal section of *Ginnungagap*'s boundary that fell proved to be anything but an isolated, fluke of an event. One after another, sections fell to the power of the flames. *Muspelheim* was succeeding in its mission; a mission that at so many times seemed fruitless. Now it was anything but as the void creaked, bent, and then broke to the deluge of fire that began pouring into it. What had once been empty and gaping abyss was now being transformed quite terribly into a waterfall of fiery rejoicing that was as close to laughing as *Muspelheim* could get.

At the exact moment when the territory-binding shield gave way to the furnace of heat that *Muspelheim* brought, the same force and rage were going on over the length of *Ginnungagap*, where yet another boundary was being torn asunder. This sort of destruction was slow and an erosion of sorts, rather than the hammer that had been swung by the flames of *Muspelheim*. The aesthetics of it all may not have been as brilliant as *Muspelheim*, nor with the flourish, but the freeze ultimately wore it down to the same effect.

With a groan and a sudden splitting crack, everything changed. The ice had been welcomed and wherever the boundary broke, the cold slipped inside and shattered it with such force that shards of melting ice splintered in all directions. That is when the two opposing worlds—fire and ice, *Muspelheim and Niflheim*—gazed upon each other, and rather than slowing or changing their forward momentum, the two forces raged on with even more ferocity. Speeding across the once-dead, rocky, cavernous void that was *Ginnungagap*, the two worlds charged toward each other with reckless abandon until finally; they met in a white-hot burst of energy.

The sky and branches above *Ginnungagap* were filled with the mist that was directed up by the impactful meeting of primordial fire and ice. Underneath, however, something was beginning to take shape in the most literal of ways. There was nothing simple, common, or normal about the inferno that had just collided with the coldest of ice; there was life itself in that burst. As the fire struck the wall of frost, droplets cascaded down into the darkest parts of *Ginnungagap*. Instead of washing away or being consumed by the earth itself, the droplets clung to one another.

What began as a small cascade was now a rushing waterfall of life-giving drops, each taking its place with the others, climbing higher and higher until there was form and shape to it. There was no longer water or fire, all that existed was flesh and blood—the very first giant, *Ymir*.

Legs the size of the thickest tree trunks stood tall and firm, each foot planted proudly in the depths of the void. Muscle piled upon muscle until the entirety of his body was towering over even the largest creatures of *Yggdrasil*. The coldest, iciest of blues met the world as his eyes opened to signal a new era of existence in the universe; *Ymir* had been created, and with that birth came the giants.

All around *Ymir* the chaos of creation was wreaking havoc on everything it touched. It was a violent battle for the territory that neither *Niflheim* nor *Muspelheim* could gain any considerable ground. Where the flames split and scorched the chasm of the void, swiftly came the ice to suffocate the fire and leave a blue tint to the ice where the inferno had been encased. The moment the ice encapsulated the spawn of *Muspelheim*, the fire returned with vengeance and melted the frozen structure of *Niflheim* until the icy cage was nothing more than a burning inferno once again.

Back and forth the war raged, *Ymir* watching all the while with wide eyes in the destruction that was giving birth to something new. Suddenly the giant heard something different than the harsh sounds that had filled his ears ever since his form was given life. He looked all about but could find nothing, yet the sound continued; a muffled bellowing—sad and haunting. The more he searched, the clearer the sound became until he turned a corner deep in the chasm of *Ginnungagap* to see a wondrous sight indeed.

Where the frost was melting away, through the rising mist, a regal beast was being created from the droplets. One by one, the droplets breathed life into each other, and when *Ymir* stumbled upon this miracle, the magnificent cow, *Audhumla*, was almost fully formed. Striking colors that seemed to shift and glimmer with every movement showed her as something more than a mere animal—she was magic and wonder and light all in one. When she finally took a step forward, the entirety of her shape was realized, *Ymir* felt something sharp and painful in his gut that sent him to his knees. His stomach was pleading for sustenance, as he had been born empty and was growing weak.

The first giant raised his head and was about to cry out when he felt a warm liquid dribble down his chin and collect in his mouth.

"What sorcery of nourishment is this?", *Ymir* thought, his mind alive with thoughts of what was happening to him. A low, gentle, silky *moo* let him know that *Audhumla* had felt his horrible pangs of hunger and didn't hesitate for a moment before her udder was bestowing the nourishment he so desperately needed.

For what seemed like an eternity *Ymir* drank the milk from *Audhumla* and slowly felt life rushing through his veins. With a soft *moo*, the cow moved to the side and laid on the cold, rocky surface, letting *Ymir* slide gently down and rest against her luxurious hide. Such exhaustion came over him like a tidal wave and he felt sleep beckoning with the pull of a yearning lover. It took no time at all for him to breathe deeply and give himself completely over to the slumber that was asking so nicely for him to join. Soon *Ymir*, the first of the giants, was asleep with his arms holding tight to the life-giving, giant-saving cow.

The fires were burning lower and the ice was reaching for less and less as the time passed and *Ymir* slept his first long sleep. All seemed calm for the first time since the borders of *Ginnungagap* broke, and yet within the silence—that was only broken for the heavy breathing of both the slumbering giant and cow—sat something terrible. There was more to come; more that needed to happen so that everything after would be possible.

Ymir hadn't so much as moved since he fell asleep, yet all of the sudden his legs began to twitch and spasm yet the tremors were contained to the legs alone, his feet didn't move one inch, nor did his hips or torso. The twitching became more of a squirming mass beneath the skin that was thrashing about trying to escape. Soundless but horrible, arms and legs pushed against the skin of *Ymir's* legs.

Faces stretched and pushed against the nearly-transparent giant's flesh until, in some dark magic, bodies began to bloodlessly tumble forth from each leg. Several from the right and several from the left made their way from the tattered flesh, and yet the moment the last one crawled from its womb-like appendage, it was as if nothing had sprung forth from either of the giant's legs. Pristine skin, untouched and unblemished; and yet not ten feet from the sleeping *Ymir* were a crowd of blinking, yawning giants. Smaller than their giant father, but still towering over anything else around them.

Ymir groaned and shifted in his sleep when both his arms moved with serpentine motions until they were straight up in the air, exposing his armpits to the air. Just as the legs had done, the skin of the giant's armpits began to tremble and stretch; the same faces and tangled arms and legs struggled to free themselves as their prior kin had done. The struggle was just as violent, yet when they spilled forth it was with the same bloodless, silent, anticlimactic manner that one would hardly shrug at it happening at all—it was a miracle of miracles.

Where there had been one giant, now there was a horde, all chattering and glancing around with their newly opened eyes. One by one they made their way off in different directions, eager to explore what this world would have to offer.

The first giant still slept soundly as though nothing at all had just occurred. His steady breathing gave no indication whatsoever of the fact that he had just birthed an entire race from within his own skin, all without the aid of being awake.

Audhumla, however, did not appreciate the disturbance and promptly got up to wander about. After lumbering about for some time, the wondrous cow came upon a massive salt lick that had been formed from the melting frost, just as she had been. Her eyes widened with excitement and her tongue lolled as she did her best to run towards the inviting, saline treat.

She took to the salt lick with reckless abandon, thinking of nothing but her desire to devour the delicious salt and enjoy every last bit. With the gigantic size of her tongue, it took very little time to make some serious headway into the salt, but then she noticed something out of the ordinary at the core of her delicious lick. This was no giant, but she was not sure *what* it was.

The power of the salt quickly shook the worry from her mind and, as cows do, she went back to enjoying her snack, each lick freeing the form inside a bit more until finally the figure, *Buri*, was freed. *Buri* was a specimen of perfection from every angle. Where earlier the creation in chaos had given birth to the first of the giants in *Ymir*, this was different. This was no giant; this was the first of the *Aesir*—the first of the gods. Sinewy arms and legs were bound in muscle, as was every part of the rest of his body. A shape designed for power with the hint of violence, even the glint in *Buri's* eyes both charmed and chilled at the same time.

Both *Niflheim* and *Muspelheim* had retreated to their worlds, but the destruction-turned-creation had already occurred. There is no way to know how long the span of time was, simply because there was no time—no night, no day, no sun or moon. Endless cycles of life turned over and over, but neither the giants nor the *Aesir* paid it any mind. Ageless wonders, they lived beside one another until slowly the bloodlines began to intermix. *Buri* had a son who he named *Bor*, and it did not take the son very long before he found a mate of his own in the giantess, *Bestla* who was the daughter of the mighty giant, *Bolthorn*.

The world maintained a sense of calm and peace in comparison to the violent and mighty collapse of *Ginnungagap*. Even though it may have seemed like there could be no further change that would send the worlds, once more, into upheaval, the reality was that there was indeed something brewing at that very moment. Hidden within the womb of

Bestla, wife of *Bor*, was the single figure who would alter everything that was and mold everything that would be in the future; *Odin* was coming.

They say that the manner of the birth will foresee the kind of child that comes from it; nothing more accurate could have been said about the event that brought three more creatures into the world. The first two children that *Bestla* bore were without complication and screamed as the world welcomed them; *Vili* and *Ve*, the half-giant, half-*Aesir* hybrids, were quiet as they looked at their mother with an almost expectant look.

Suddenly, *Bestla* screamed from her soul as pain tore through her. Stabbing, grinding, ripping, searing agony made her throw her head back and cry out in the deepest, darkest tongue. Violent tremors wracked her body as *Odin* made his way into the world, not so much welcomed, but he reached out for the world from within. His brothers watched as their mother gave birth to the one who would bring about everything that would come.

Standing tall, covered in blood, and wearing a horrifying smile, *Odin* was already fully formed and had a deep, burning desire to seek out something bigger than himself—something that would give him true power. When you are born with a gaping hole inside you that can only be filled with absolute, unquestionable power, every single action and breath is focused on that one, singular need. Calling out to both *Vili* and *Ve*, the three brothers left their mother sobbing and panting, as she truly believed her children would destroy her during their birth.

"Odin, where are you taking us, our brother?" asked *Ve*, meekly staring out from behind his brother, *Vili* as the three rested for a moment. They had been walking for quite a time without a word passing amongst them and curiosity was getting the better of the eldest but smallest of them, *Ve*. Odin turned slowly and simply stared at his brothers, not harshly but with a soft affection.

"As I was being shown the way into this world through our mother, I was given a dream. I saw a world created by us—with our own hands. We fashioned mountains and skies and seas and rain. It was ours to decide, and ours to create."

"Could we really do such a thing, brother," ventured *Vili*, who was getting more excited by the minute as he heard *Odin*'s words, "We are new to this world and unaware of its many offerings. Who are we to birth and create?"

"Why not us, brothers?" *Odin* stood tall and spread his arms wide, "The rest of the creatures simply live and breed and live some more, but there is no purpose, no drive, no *true life* to be found. This is why you are with me because I have been shown the way to be better and to make this scarred, ashen place something precious that could give life rather than just exist within it.

"There is a cost, though, as the dream also showed me. None of this can come from nothing, and so we must seek out the mightiest objects we can find, and the vision told me that from its form, we shall have the tools to be creators of life and worlds! All that you need to do is follow me, and when we get where we need to be, follow my lead once more."

His two brothers stood in shock and awe, enamored by the vision *Odin* had just laid out to them, and with a dual cheer, they were bound to the vision *Odin* had spoken.

The trio followed the pull and tug that *Odin* had in his core all over the charred ground that had been the void. Smoldering ash piles displayed where the turmoil between fire and ice had waged, now only memories and silence. After quite some time, they finally came upon the source of the burning inside *Odin*, the target for his yearning; *Ymir*. When *Odin* gazed upon the first and mightiest of the giants, he did not see a foe or a worthy opponent. Instead, he saw an offering that needed to be torn apart and reshaped into something worthwhile; he saw the cost of creation.

Odin had no explanation for why he had been brought into the world with this need, but he never questioned it. Many had come before him, and yet the future had tapped him on the shoulder and granted him with this vision. He was told there was a cost. Was *Ymir* it? There must be a reason why this beast of a giant stood in his way. The mind can do amazing things when justification is needed, and *Odin*'s was working overtime.

"This giant, this beast, is dangerous and if we leave it to its own affairs, it will soon turn on the *Aesir* and all our brothers and sisters." He whispered to his brothers, a hand on each of their shoulders. *Odin*'s eyes were wide and unblinking as he was locked onto the massive giant.

As though he had been appointed the protector of the creatures in the charred remains of the void, he waited motionless for ages upon ages until finally, *Ymir* fell into a deep slumber. Not wanting to charge in error, he patiently waited until the giant had snored fifty times and then without further wait the three snuck forward in silence. As they crept closer and closer to the slumbering mound that was *Ymir*, *Odin* stooped down and examined rock after rock until he found three that were solid, heavy, and sharp to the touch. The fire had honed these three stones as though this was their very purpose—to kill *Ymir*.

The first giant, *Ymir*, had almost no time to react as the three figures leaped upon his neck and began hacking away at his throat with violent fervor. *Odin* began laughing a high-pitched, shriek-like laugh as he sent flesh, blood, and bone scattering in all directions. It was over so quickly that the giant's mouth and eyes were still agape in surprise and horror at the way his life was ending.

Dripping from head to toe in blood, *Odin* kept sawing away until he was able to hold the head of *Ymir* in his hands. He had never felt this surge of power as he was experiencing at that moment, and something told him to hold the head high into the sky. As he did, raising his arms and the dismembered head, a bright burst of light caused him to drop his arms to cover his eyes but the head stayed rising through the air.

The blinding light began to envelop it until there was nothing but white. Then, as quick as it arrived, the light was gone. The three stared up where the head just disappeared with enormous eyes and slack jaws. Instead of the absolute black that had always been overhead, suddenly there were blue and wisps of white above them. As they breathed in, it was like the first breath their lungs had ever taken—full and fresh, unhindered and without suffocation.

"Brothers," *Odin* said, turning to *Ve* and *Vili* with a broad grin, "Let us create!"

So it was that the world's creation truly began. The head of the giant *Ymir* became the rounded dome of the sky with his brains swirling into clouds, his skin was stretched over the scorched ground to create the earth, they mixed his blood and sweat to create the oceans, his long hair became massive, luscious forests with green and brown trees, and *Odin* used the bones of the first and mightiest giant to form the ranges of mountains that line the world.

He had been born with many purposes and the first was now complete, but the slayer of giants, *Odin*, had much more to do still—but all in good time.

CHAPTER TWO:

ODIN'S CRUELTY: SUN AND MOON, NIGHT AND DAY

*O*din woke from his sleep with a dreadful scream and drenched in sweat, just as he had done the last three nights. He was being haunted in every dream by those looming branches; *Yggdrasil* was calling to him. *Odin* had been born with the desperate need for knowledge already in his veins, and the vision he received as he clawed his way out of his mother only deepened that appetite. He had caught a glimpse of something no other being had been shown, but that was just it. Despite all the wonder and glory that had come from it, the vision remained a mere glimpse and he wanted more.

Odin wanted everything.

The months following the three brothers' creation of the world had been a whirlwind of power, fantastical magic, and more creating of beings and shapes and all manner of things. *Odin* formed dwarves from the maggots swarming inside the tattered and emptied corpse of *Ymir* but that was not enough. He wanted there to be no mistaking the order of power, so once the dwarves were created, he chose four to stand at the corners of his formed world. Not to guard or stand watch, but to be a reminder that nothing was greater than *Odin* and nothing was outside of his grasp.

The more he dug into the power he wielded, the more he wanted and the greater it had to be. So, for all eternity, the four dwarves—*Austri, Vestri, Nordri,* and *Sudri*—existed as a glaring example that all creation was owned by *Odin* and he could do as he pleased.

It may seem as though *Odin's* cruelty in creation was simply that and nothing more, but the truth ran much deeper. His violent birth had scarred him with a need for knowledge, ever more and always seeking, and yet he had been unable to find a source in this bleak place he had been brought into. All the forming of the world was for naught in his eyes, because every single piece of it was made as a cry into the void, desperate to get an answer from *Yggdrasil* about where he needed to go to find the next taste of knowledge.

He had torn the body of the first giant asunder to get the attention of whoever or whatever deemed it necessary to bring him into existence, but he was only ever answered with silence.

He wanted to give in to the growing exhaustion in his heart, but the pull of his desire was much stronger than his weakness. As strained and emptied as he felt, he didn't stop creating, even when it was excruciating to do so. In everything, though, he was sure to never let anyone outside his own mind know of his struggles. He was not just a being, not just a god, he was the creator and the only one who could take control over the chaos that had ruled without challenge. Well, here he was now to challenge it and rip it from the hands of the darkness.

Odin returned to the festering body of *Ymir* and with inspiration to build more, something wondrous that would be impossible for *Yggdrasil* to ignore. He wanted something special that would be greater than all his creations before because this time he would do it for himself and those ever loyal to him. The void created the giants in a whirlwind of power and might in the first few breaths of its existence, and every time *Odin* looked at one, he felt disgust twisting inside of him.

From the moment he felt the ability to create within himself, *Odin* wanted to make something strong, perfect, and beautiful—as he was. It was less of inspiration and more defiance because all around him he saw lumbering examples of how, when left to its own, the universe could not be trusted to create. When he gazed upon the sky and mountains that he and his brothers had formed, he saw a wondrous landscape, but dotting the greens and grays were the towering creatures that the void had haphazardly brought into being and he felt it all being tainted.

As much as he didn't want to admit it, the giants had grown beyond his reach and it caused him many nights of worry. For all his power there were much, much more of them than there were of him—even if he would be defended by his brothers. The spirit of the brother's kinship was less protective and more parasitic, and so Odin always doubted he would be saved by their heroics if it came down to it.

For a brief, fleeting moment, he felt powerless and nearly willed himself to sink into the ground and remain encased in rock rather than see the scourge of giants overwhelm the world he was trying to beautify. That only lasted for a second, and then he felt his confidence return as he could see what he was finally destined to do; create. This time, though, he felt more purpose and intent behind his vision as he saw what was left of *Ymir's* corpse and no longer saw decay, but promise instead.

The first task that *Odin* undertook was to follow the pull he felt on his spirit, leading him to two fallen logs lying beside one another. To anyone else, they appeared to be nothing more than some wood, but *Odin* saw something more—much more. The giants were the children of the void, but the world around them was of his own design, so it only made sense that he also brings forth offspring of his own. He despised the misshapen forms that the giants held, so he took inspiration from himself when he began to create. Upon completion, *Odin* had fashioned two figures from the logs; one made from an ash tree, the other from an elm.

Lifeless, they stood frozen, each one an homage to its creator yet unable to whisper a word of praise. *Odin* was overwhelmed with satisfaction as he looked over each of the figures, naming them as he did so. One he called *Ask*, after the ash tree he had derived him from, and the other he named *Embla*, for the elm she had been formed from. With the closest thing he could feel to love, his fingers brushed each of their faces, and where once were statues, now stood living, breathing beings— his humans.

Odin was not fully prepared for how he would feel when he looked upon the two creations of his, but he knew he wanted them safe from the only other thing in his world that could threaten them; the giants. He called upon his brothers and between the three of them; they dug deeper into the corpse of *Ymir* and built a separate world for these humans— *Midgard*. All around the human world was a mighty fortress built from the eyelashes of the first giant, and each one designed with the explicit purpose of keeping the giants out of *Midgard*. He imbued the very stones and dirt themselves with that same purpose; it was all to keep *Ask* and *Embla* protected. Well, that is not entirely true, because, beneath the adoration for his creations and the purpose he held for that moment, the core intent of the entire event was to send out a plea so loud, so magical, and so strong that there was no way *Yggdrasil* could ignore him any longer.

Odin was not simply a creator anymore; he was a father and a protector, even if it was all done in pursuit of his desires. He was sure that once he did all of this, the voice of the ancient tree would speak to him and lead him, but there was only the same awful silence that he had been met with day after day, and time after time.

If the creator had a heart to break, at that moment, it would have shattered. Everything had felt like a waste and where he once stowed warmth in his soul, now the icy fingers of anger were creeping back into the spotlight. Everything around him that had been beautiful now looked unappealing and empty. He no longer cared what happened to those beings he had brought into the world, nor for the giants or anything else. He felt as if something inside him had broken, and the only true sentiments left was rage—uncontrollable, unquenchable rage.

When the master of creation finally gave in to exhaustion, his dreams became more and more vivid; each one painting a picture of everything he desired, but the one thing he truly *needed* was always just beyond his grasp. Forever and a day could have been spent forming and creating endlessly, but *Odin* was not remotely satisfied with this because it was not the power he desired, but the knowledge that crouched behind power, giving it strength and purpose. He knew that power alone was fleeting, but if he knew everything, then there would be no end to what he could accomplish.

The problem was that the dreams turned into haunting nightmares he couldn't escape from. He searched all over the cavernous landscape of the mountains to the cascading waterfalls, but there was no more knowledge than when he had first been granted the deeper sight—if only for that glimpse. The more he dreamed of what he couldn't have, the crueler he became.

For a time, though none remain to speak of it, four nearly inseparable beings watched over all of *Odin's* creation with calm and compassionate eyes. The sun and moon, a sister and brother, named *Mani* and *Sol*, laughed at each other's jokes without end, one lighting up as the other dimmed, and then again, they would switch. No struggle, no differing; just siblings who enjoyed the presence of each other.

The other pair of the foursome was the night and day, *Nott* and *Dag*. *Nott*, the dark giantess, had come into this world already with a son in her arms and a fiery love for him in her soul. *Dag*, full of energy and spirit, was everything to her and she loved nothing more than watching him shine brightly over the land while *Sol* smiled beside him. She hummed a gentle song when he slept and let the light rest a while as *Mani* took her watch. This was beauty at its finest, but as was said earlier, it was only for a short while.

The cruelty of *Odin* was spreading like a raging wildfire, engulfing everything in its path. He struck down beings and rebuilt them only to destroy them once again, but when that did nothing to ease his emptiness inside, he burned for something harsher, something that would bring a smile to even his stony face. The worst moments come from unfortunate coincidences, and as *Odin* was trying to think of something truly terrible to distract him from his nightmares, there came the peal of laughter from above him. In all his anger he had completely forgotten about the four beings he had charged with watching over the light and dark, but in an instant, he was reminded in the worst possible way.

Looking upward he saw a joyful display that caused his teeth to grind. Here he was without fulfillment and without the means to take his purpose, and yet these four were parading their joy around as if to flaunt it directly in his face. What was to the four above him a horrific occurrence was meant to be in the mind of *Odin*. He was all-powerful and nothing could surpass him, so the moment he wanted to destroy something beautiful, he was given precisely that without a moment's delay. Fate had lined this up perfectly for him, so of course, he was going to take full advantage of it.

Odin was in prime form, which meant that destruction was too easy and much too clean for this particular moment. He wanted this to last, which meant he had to be more creative than usual. As of late, his signature move had been crushing a throat or tearing out a heart—both of which he could undo and then do over again multiple times—but even the bloodiest of acts were getting a bit mundane. Perhaps a bloodless approach would be more appropriate; he wanted to purge the joy from their souls, not just hurt them. The punishment for flaunting what he couldn't have was going to be torture of the most devious kind.

Nott was doing the thing she loved most; watching her son smile. If, just for a moment, something other than happiness touched her heart, all she had to do was to look upon *Dag* and there would be nothing but warmth and love cultivating within her. The day had been as usual, but for some reason, the darkness of her realm—the night—was not the same as it always was. That was when she glanced down and saw the most frightening sight ever; *Odin* was looking directly up, not at her, but at her son who was still smiling as he slept. She couldn't hear what the creator was murmuring, but she saw his mouth moving, and then in one awful, drawn-out minute, everything became a hellish scene of pain and suffering.

For a second, she thought the darkness was blurring her vision, but it wasn't a trick—her son was moving away from her. At first, it was a gradual act, but gradually he flew further and further away from her.

Panicked, she went to scream, but only silence followed, her mouth and eyes agape as she realized she could not move. In her mind, the world was filled with her cries, each one a desperate plea for *Odin* to stop taking her son from her. She tried again to call out *Dag's* name but nothing came from her mouth—not even a strained whisper. Before she knew it, he was gone, over the horizon and out of her sight for the first time.

Born with him in her arms, now the piece that made her life worthwhile had been taken away from her and the pain was astronomical. As if the act itself wasn't enough, suddenly she could speak again, and the sound of her cries were heard for miles and miles. She sobbed and choked, screamed, and dug her nails into her face until it bled. She was still frozen in place, but that swiftly changed, and as soon as she was able, she raced through the sky to where her son had disappeared, but he was nowhere to be seen. That was when she heard the cackling, awful voice of *Odin* from below.

"Chase him! Perhaps if you're fast enough you can still catch him before he wakes," He paused for a moment, allowing his words to sink in because the only thing worse than her own pain was the pain her son would feel when he woke without her, "I would guess that he is going to be scared to not see you for, what, the first time? That would definitely be a frightening experience, so I would hurry."

Nott tried to pick up speed but even though she was moving, it was at a consistent pace; one she now knew was controlled by the beastly creator below. Soon after, the sky was filled with screams of her son; Dag was awake and terrified. She called out to him and he answered, but she could still not see him. For what seemed like an eternity, she chased, never gaining or losing speed, just maintaining at the same pace. Her throat was ragged and she could barely hear *Dag* for the hoarseness in his as well. As she looked down, she realized something that caused her heart to stop beating for a fraction of a moment—she had come full circle.

The place where she started when *Odin* first sent her son from her was now beneath her again, which meant she raced the entire way around the world and still hadn't found him, and yet, as quiet as it was, she still heard his cries off in the distance. A sinking feeling in her soul came right before the full realization hit her; she wasn't meant to find him, nor see him. She was moving at a pace that he probably was as well, keeping her from him. There was nothing inside her now; not fear or anger or sorrow, just emptiness. She was numb. There had been no warning and no reasoning, only the need for something cruel and horrible to happen. She had simply been there, enjoying the simplicity of her existence, only to now reside here in this hell.

There was a part of *Odin*—some untainted, more compassionate part—that assumed once he sent mother and son forever in a hellish cycle of sorrow, it would alleviate at least some of his inner aching. Instead, all he felt was a deeper burning in his chest, and fire flowed through his veins. He had gotten used to the simple trade-offs since the world had been formed; an act of cruelty bought him a moment's distraction, at least.

Sometimes he would bask in the gargantuan horror of the act just to squeeze a few more moments of peace from it. This was different, though, because he barely felt a flutter of the distraction he had come to expect. It was replaced with an anxious, twitching, dull buzzing throughout his being.

"It isn't fair," he said through gritted teeth, his jaw creaking from the pressure he was forcing upon his own structure, "I had no choice, no choice at all." He was pacing now, striding long, determined paces as the mournful figures of night and day passed above him, forever seeking the other without hope. *Odin* preferred the simpler aspects of this world he brought into being and this underlying layer of need that he had was anything but simple. He wanted to rid himself of such cravings and simply exist, but every waking thought and nightmare orbited the same beckoning voice that called to him. It was soft but firm, melodic, and destructive at the same time without ever encroaching on the other; absolute harmony.

Yggdrasil never stopped reaching out to him, each time with more fervor and pull than before. It was a part of him he longed to deny, but it was so ingrained into his soul that there was no way to separate the one from the other; *Odin* didn't just want knowledge, he needed it. It had been a yearning at the start, but each day he felt more and more empty, and the buzzing in his head became more prominent each moment that he didn't discover that ever-elusive knowledge. It was out there, where *Yggdrasil* was calling to him from, but right now it existed only in his mind.

Odin was prepared to set off from where he had torn son from mother when he heard muffled voices coming from behind a rocky outcrop. He slowly crept over and peered around the stones to see two huddled forms trying their best to be invisible against the cold gray of the rocks. He had nearly forgotten about the siblings that had been practically inseparable from *Nott* and *Dag*—before *Odin* had his way, at least—and yet here they were, too scared to even run. The brother, *Sol*, turned and with as firm a look as he could muster, spoke in a halting, nervous manner.

"Leave us be, I beg you," A shudder of a breath took his words for a moment before he could continue, "Two of our dearest ones you sent away into the sky. Surely that is enough and we can be ignored. You will never need to think of us again."

Odin knew there was some truth in what the boy said because he could just leave and there would be nothing for the worse. The thought of the siblings would probably never cross his mind, if ever, and yet he was not in the best of moods. Taking his rage out on these two would not solve his quest towards *Yggdrasil*, but considering everything he had tried to do to get the tree's attention, perhaps something more in line with his nature would be louder than his prior attempts.

"I see you were trying to hide," *Odin* began, letting his voice soften just enough so that *Sol's* sister, *Mani*, glanced up for a moment. "It wouldn't be from me, would it?" Of course, it was from him, but that wasn't the point. He needed this—them—to be a conduit for all the anger and disappointment that was building within him. He wanted it to be a beacon of cruelty that *Yggdrasil* could follow to him and realize that this was no giant or man that was crying out—it was *Odin*.

"After what happened with our friends, you can see why we fled and did our best to hide. Fear is not in our nature; we are meant for joy." *Sol* had meant to calm *Odin* with these words but he happened to do quite the opposite, for hearing that these meaningless things were experiencing and living in joy each day was more than he could bear hearing. Day after day he trudged through a world that was lesser than he, searching for knowledge only to be ignored; if anyone deserved that kind of joy, surely it was him and not these two shivering weaklings.

"Well, there are much worse things out there than I," he said to the siblings, a false smile on his face. For all the things that *Odin* had pieced together in creation, he was particularly fond of one; the wolf. He found some strange comfort in the sleek form, the terrifying rows of teeth, and the hunter's spirit. All his endless wandering and searching had been put into these beasts, so they roamed always in search of more to devour. As *Odin* finished his sentence, he gave a quiet whistle that seemed to echo and carry across the rocks and over the grass up into the sky where *Nott* sorrowfully floated.

"What things?" *Sol* asked, just as the rumbling of a growl could be heard behind *Odin*. As the creator stepped aside, he revealed a panting, ravenous pack of wolves, each staring directly at the huddled siblings. As *Odin* stood there smiling at the pale, terrified faces of both brother and sister, he held his hand up, and the wolves all sat as one, closed mouths and patient eyes.

"Are you ready?" *Odin* asked, looking from *Sol* to *Mani* and then back to the wolves.

"Ready?" *Sol's* voice was again trembling.

"Run. Run and hide." His timbre was deep, and the pacing of his words was excruciatingly slow. For a moment neither of the siblings moved, but then *Sol* hurriedly got his sister to her feet and they took off under the cover of the night, away from where *Odin* was still holding the wolves at bay with nothing but his raised hand. He gave a small chuckle as he began counting down, giving the siblings a chance to at least locate a new hiding spot.

Off in the distance, where the brother and sister had hidden, came a soft glow, and then it turned into a bright, shining light. At first, it was stationary, then it split itself into two beams and began moving about from one place to another in jagged, zig-zag patterns. Each time the lights jerked back and forth, *Odin* gave a low laugh, one that was meant only for himself and the wolves, who were still waiting tensely, staring back and forth from their master's hand to the dancing lights in the distance. The further the lights travelled, the brighter they shone. There was no place for them to hide from anything, let alone something as brutally built for the chase as the wolves were.

Sol stared in horror at his skin as it glowed and shone brilliantly, giving him no chance to shield himself or his sister. From rock to rock they ran, imagining that by huddling over they somehow dimmed the cursed light that was bursting from their bodies. They knew it was only a matter of time until *Odin* grew tired and his hand lowered, meaning the wolves would have no barrier between them and the two figures glowing on the horizon.

In a blind panic, he suddenly remembered where their other two dear friends were—lost to the skies, but at least *Nott* and *Dag* were safe, even if they were forever alone. Maybe if they took to the skies, he and his sister could hide among the stars—the only thing that remained from the volcanic sparks when fire met ice.

Grabbing his sister's hand and closing his eyes, he focused all his willpower and blasted off from the earth. As the two traversed higher and higher, it seemed for a moment as if this plan would work and they had found an escape. A smile even began to creep across *Mani's* face, but it fell immediately as she let out a horrible scream and pointed behind her brother to where the pack of wolves was storming towards them. *Sol* went to calm her because they couldn't catch them up here, but then his voice caught in his throat as one by one the wolves flew into the air and ever faster towards them. In a blur of fur and teeth and snarling jaws, he was shoved aside and trampled by the many hustling paws of the wolves.

He heard his sister screaming, and then it got fainter and fainter until he couldn't hear it at all. He forced his battered eyes open and looked around, only to see that his sister and the wolves were nowhere to be seen, except for the faintest glow on the very edge of the horizon. In a panic, he realized that they were still chasing her, but he didn't even have time to process that thought when *Odin*, who had only released a few of his wolf pack, let the others race off into the dark night sky after the stunned *Sol*.

Odin watched as his wolves chased the boy off through the sky into the distance until he disappeared over the horizon, just as his sister had done. He stood for a while looking into the sky until he heard the sound he had been waiting for; the screams of *Mani*. Across the sky she went, the wolves behind her, more ravenous than before and keeping pace all the while.

This was justice in his eyes; it was his creation, his world, and he would not simply stand by while they experienced something that he only ever seemed to chase—joy. More than that, though, he was hoping deep inside himself that this was finally enough to catch the attention of the only thing that could fulfil his needs; *Yggdrasil*. Pleading hadn't worked, creating and power hadn't done a thing, so perhaps cruelty—unabashed, dark cruelty—would finally do the job.

"Is this enough?" He roared, looking all around him, "What more could you possibly need to see before you give me what I need?" He knew that knowledge, true knowledge, required a sacrifice, and isn't that what he had been doing? He sacrificed *Ymir*, then his own creation, and despite all of it, he was still here; shouting at nothing and receiving nothing in return. He felt his blood become heated, and he began to tremble from the anger that was filling him from soul to flesh to mind.

He felt tricked, as though he had been brought into this world as a mockery of power instead of something truly powerful. Given that brief taste of something as wondrous as knowledge—precious, secret knowledge given only to him—and now he was hungry and there was nothing to satiate that yearning.

CHAPTER THREE:

ODIN'S SACRIFICE FOR KNOWLEDGE

*O*din, exhausted by his desperate cries, finally collapsed to the ground in a sweating, panting heap. He felt as though he had nothing left to give because every single thing he had done was in pursuit of something that was nowhere to be found. As he laid his head on the cold ground, he was surrounded by a booming voice.

"Odin, creator and destroyer, why do you seek me?"

There was only one other time when *Odin* had heard that voice before and it was still as clear as it had been on that day. His birth had been bloody and violent, even so, the one thing he remembered more than anything was that voice; *Yggdrasil*

"You know why I have sought you!" *Odin's* voice was wavering slightly because, for the first time, he felt the presence of something greater than himself. He felt the experience and age in every word that was spoken to him and in another first he discovered what it was like to respect someone other than himself. It was as though it was finally all worth it, and yet he still felt so far from his goal, "You let me taste knowledge for a moment, and though it was a moment of brilliance that has led me my entire life, it was not enough. Not nearly enough."

He didn't mean for his voice to become quieter, but the more he spoke, the more he realized who he was speaking to. He knew the opportunity that was before him and still one of the few things he could think of was that such a thing—a wondrous thing—as *Yggdrasil* had no reason to pay him any mind. When the universe and everything in and around it dies, *Yggdrasil* would still be there watching time go by without a care. All the knowledge in the world was encased in that mighty trunk and blossoming out into the branches.

"And what have you done to earn such a thing? Knowledge is not for all, it is not for the usual or the weak—what have you done?"

"I have sacrificed!"

"Sacrificed what, Odin? Yourself? Because I see no evidence of that. You have let others step in front of you and take the blade, each time using it to your own ends. You did all this in your own name, and dare to cry out to me afterward?"

Odin had no answer to this because it genuinely rang true, even though he desperately wanted it to be a lie thrown about by an ancient being attempting to skirt the issue. Instead, here he was, being forced to face a reality that meant many things, all of them horrible. Had he truly given nothing of himself? He couldn't possibly question the words of

Yggdrasil, especially when he was able to feel its power all around him. Finally, after what felt like an eternity of silence, *Odin* spoke.

"What then, *Yggdrasil*, can I give of myself? What sacrifice will bring me what I desire?"

Everything became white. He heard nothing and could see nothing except for that blinding white all around and then slowly—ever so slowly—the white started to transition into other shades and shapes until it was very clear that he was no longer standing underneath the same sky as he had been. Instead, he was on his knees staring up at the largest thing he had ever seen, or could ever possibly imagine.

He had always wondered what the Tree of Wisdom would look like when he finally could find it, but nothing could have prepared him for the sheer size of it. He couldn't see the highest branches, nor could he gaze around its base, which stretched forever in all directions. Mist drifted about as the different shapes were still coming into focus as his sight slowly returned.

Somehow, he had been transported here, with *Yggdrasil*, but that was not all he saw. Stags fed along the base of the tree, a squirrel rapidly clawed its way up the tree chattering away and soon after came streaking down to chatter some more. It was a place alive and abundant with an energy unlike anything he had ever felt, but with each passing second, he felt as if he did not belong here. He had always considered himself the height of strength and power, meant to rule and create, but here he simply felt small; dwarfed next to the staggering height that *Yggdrasil's* branches reached.

"Where is your power now, Odin?"

The ancient tree was right because *Odin* felt something he had never had before; true powerlessness. Not a single spark of strength was felt in any part of his body, and that sent a chill down to his core.

"What has all your cruelty brought you? You deceived yourself in believing that your actions were necessary and would somehow bring you closer to me? To knowledge? Do you feel closer now?"

"No," *Odin's* voice had never been as quiet as it was at that moment. He felt like a child being scolded, but so much worse. In a second, this powerful being could remove him entirely from existence. Forgotten in the worst possible way.

"You must find what true sacrifice is, or else knowledge will always be just outside your grasp. You will live forever knowing that you are less than you could be, all because the sacrifice wasn't something you could reach."

"How do I find true sacrifice?" *Odin* yelled up into the branches, unsure of where to direct his voice, "What do you mean?" The voice had faded, though, and all he was left with was the animals who had also stopped to turn their eyes to him as though waiting to see what his next move may be.

His mind was running wild, trying to think of how he was to show *Yggdrasil* that he truly was worthy and everything before was simply the errors that had led him to this moment. He had to figure out what true sacrifice was because up until now he had gotten it wrong in every possible way. *Yggdrasil* was absolutely correct, but what would be a way to sacrifice part of himself?

That is when the idea struck *Odin* like a thunderbolt; it wasn't enough to sacrifice *part* of himself. The more he thought about it, the more he realized that if he wasn't able to obtain knowledge then any life he would have from here on would be worthless and a menial struggle through disappointment. That was not the journey for *Odin*, not for the one who created the world and formed humans, built the sky and mountains, and—cruel as it was—made day and night, sun and moon, eternally cycle. He was meant for more, and if it meant being willing to give everything else up it would be more than worthwhile.

He looked around for something that would serve his purposes and for a time he worried nothing would suit his intent here, but then he saw something that seemed as though it had been formed precisely for his need. A long branch somehow was growing upwards from the base of *Yggdrasil's* trunk, ending in a needle-like point, as though the tree had grown a spear. It was sturdy and almost seemed to be waiting for something; *Odin* knew what it was waiting for, and he didn't hesitate a moment more. Taking a deep breath, he screamed out to *Yggdrasil*.

"If you desire sacrifice, then you will receive a worthy sacrifice, for a life without knowledge is not one I wish to live!" He launched himself into the air and impaled himself on the spear, doing his best to ignore the searing pain as it pushed its way through him, leaving him hanging and bleeding from it, red streaks cascading down onto the grass by the trunk.

Odin was sure that once *Yggdrasil* witnessed his sacrifice, he would immediately be saved and everything he had ever wanted would be his. That is why he was so shocked when hours passed, his pain endless and his breathing ragged, and still *Yggdrasil* had not said a thing. As if they wanted to make a point also, the animals had moved away from him so that he was truly alone. He tried to wriggle and undo this obvious mistake, but it was to no avail. He had done too good a job when he speared himself, and now he was stuck.

After the first day went by, *Odin* was lost in a haze of pain and regret as he hung from the branch, dried blood all around him. The minutes were passing slower than he had ever felt before, in a way that seemed to grind upon his every nerve. Then the second day passed, then the third, and still *Odin* hung in silence without *Yggdrasil* uttering a single word. He had completely lost hope that this would favorably, and yet somewhere deep inside he wondered if this was simply what his eternity looked like. Never spoken to, never looked upon, just impaled upon a spear forever without hope of attaining the knowledge he had so desperately sought.

By the time the ninth day came, *Odin* was locked in a chamber inside his mind, doing all he could to escape from the reality he had created for himself. He was focused on staying there and nothing could change his mind. That is until he once again heard that booming, powerful, all-encompassing voice.

"I have seen many things since the universe brought me into it," *Odin* was almost too lost in his head, but the more *Yggdrasil* spoke, the more *Odin* allowed himself to creep out from his protected place inside. ***"I did not think this would be one of the things I saw, for you now understand what sacrifice is. True sacrifice, for you were willing to give everything of yourself up simply because you believed that much in what you were seeking. Even if you had no guarantee that you would succeed, here you hang. I am not surprised often, but this time I truly am."***

Odin felt himself rising and he watched in amazement as the spear left his body and his feet finally touched the ground after what felt like an eternity. His breath returned to him just as it had been before as if he had never been pierced by the spear like branch. When he looked at his chest it was true, for there was not even a scar to show where he had hung for the longest nine days he had ever experienced.

"Why—why did you do this for me?" *Odin* was still getting his voice back so he hoarsely choked out the words, "What was different?"

"You gave yourself, and that is what was missing before. Now, you have shown why you are worthy of what you have been seeking."

Before *Odin* could answer, his head was filled with more thoughts than he had in his entire lifetime combined; each one eve more unique and special than the thought before. Knowledge cascaded into his mind like welcomed rain, watering the dry fields of his intellect. He was shown images of runes, writings, visions, and everything else that *Yggdrasil* had coursing through itself.

Slowly, *Yggdrasil* poured knowledge into *Odin*, showing him things no one else had ever seen or ever would see. Before it was all done, something slipped through the cracks that he was never supposed to see. The mighty tree had missed it as the knowledge fell forth. *Odin* saw a world on fire; gods and giants battling, blood flowing like rivers across the world he had created. Wolves tore at flesh and the mightiest of them all, *Fenrir*, burst forth and joined the fray. Suddenly, in the mud made red with blood, was a body that looked all too familiar. He let out an audible gasp as he saw the face; it was the face of a fallen *Odin*, eyes clouded and life gone.

When the vision ended, he could barely catch his breath. He was bent over, his hands gripping his knees tightly as he tried to slow the world from spinning around him. How would that happen? Surely, he couldn't be killed, but perhaps he had missed something. Maybe he wasn't as powerful as he thought, but nothing mattered if this was true. He would meet his end one day, and when that was, he had no possible clue, but he had been given a high cost to the knowledge he sought. More costly than hanging for days on a spear or enduring the cruelty he had caused; to be forced to confront mortality you didn't know existed was a horror he wouldn't wish on anyone. He didn't even know how to fully process it, though the image would surely be forever ingrained into his mind.

One day he would die.

CHAPTER FOUR:

BALDUR

Years had passed since *Odin* envisioned his own form lying lifelessly on the blood-soaked ground. Since then, the world had drastically changed, all done with the craftsmanship of the creator himself. *Odin* was now more than just a powerful being. He was the chieftain of the gods, ruling over sons, daughters, friends, and other mighty beings that all lived in the magnificent world he had constructed for them—*Asgard.*

Odin was the closest thing that *Yggdrasil* had to a peer, and as such, he was given the freedom to build high into the branches. Worlds for elves and dwarves, fire and ice, all-encompassing the mighty tree, and all were now calm and contained thanks to the work *Odin* had achieved. He could never be described as a compassionate soul, but he was indeed a changed being compared to the beast that roamed the world desiring for nothing but chaos and pain.

As the gods populated, *Odin* began building *Asgard* in the highest place in *Yggdrasil* he could find. He ruled from a grand throne with a raven on each of his shoulders. The first raven, *Hugin*, represented his thoughts, while the other, *Mumin*, held his memories. Each day, they departed from his sides and circled the world to gather more knowledge for their master. As changed as he was, as calm as his soul had become, his thirst for knowledge had not dissipated one bit. One would think that all that *Yggdrasil* had given to him would be enough for fifty lifetimes, but *Odin* ended each day with his two ravens bestowing even more of the world's knowledge into his mind.

Of all the gods he ruled over, one of his favorites was his own son, *Baldur*. The creator's son was the product of *Odin* and the sorceress goddess, *Frigg*, who was known for her kind heart and compassion for all. There was no god as beloved and well-thought of as *Baldur*. It didn't matter who it was, when *Baldur* was around there was more life and a brighter atmosphere.

Everything was perfect in *Odin's* world, and sadly that is usually when the worst moments tend to arrive.

It all began with a nightmare. *Odin* awoke covered in sweat and teary-eyed; he had seen his son murdered. It was so painful that he didn't return to bed for the rest of the night. Unfortunately, the next night the same thing happened, and the night after that. For days on end, he awoke to horrible dreams of how his son would die, each one bloodier and more gruesome than the last. After two weeks of the same horrific images, he'd had enough.

"I'm telling you, *Frigg*," *Odin* said as he paced the spacious throne room from one end to the next, "These dreams mean something. I have never had so many of the same visions one after the next; it is trying to tell me something."

Frigg had gotten used to not responding when he was in this kind of state because he would continue to ramble on and on before finding the answer himself soon enough. It was something learned over years, and it saved her a great deal of grief—not to mention several arguments. Right on cue, he broke the silence with a response to all of his concerns.

"And yes, I tried to call out to *Yggdrasil,* but apparently he doesn't want to get involved!" The last part was shouted to the ceiling as if that would somehow get the mighty tree to answer him. "Not a word. I first assumed the dreams were coming from him, as the mighty tree can send messaging in mysterious ways, but the lack of an answer leaves me to think it must be something else."

More silence as he conversed within his head, even though he spoke directly towards *Frigg.*

"It must mean something though, and if this is yet another prophecy meant to haunt me, I shall not sit back and do nothing! I may not be able to change what lies ahead for myself, but I'll be damned if I will stand by while my son's life is in danger!"

Frigg watched on, worry all over her face, as *Odin* stormed from the throne room calling for anyone who could hear that he needed his horse. Perhaps she wouldn't have been as concerned if he had just requested any horse because then he wouldn't have been expecting danger and risk, but her heart sank when she heard *Odin* ordered the marshal to saddle his most trusted steed, *Sleipnir.*

As quickly as she could go, the goddess ran from the throne room and didn't stop until she caught the arm of *Odin* as he was about to mount his horse.

"Where are you going in such a state?" She wanted to tell him to stay, but she knew better and let her eyes speak what she could not.

"If *Yggdrasil* decides to remain silent, there is but one seeress who can offer me the sight I require to know if my son is safe or whether he must be protected!"

Again, her heart fell because she knew exactly of who he spoke. *Odin* was heading to the underworld to speak to the one and only, the seeress of the dead. Long ago she perished and so great was her power that she holds a position among the underworld and the souls within it.

Frigg had heard tales of what *Odin* had survived and knew of the powers he wielded, but even still, she worried that this would be the last time she saw him. There was no guarantee that he would return, nor was there a sure safe passage once he was beneath the earth. He let his eyes linger on hers and then galloped off, the hooves of *Sleipnir* throwing dirt in all directions as they sped away.

Odin was not only a creator, but he could also take on many disguises so that he could move about freely without contest, and on this occasion, he chose his best cover to hide his true identity. If those in the underworld knew that he was roaming around their world trying to gain even more knowledge, there would be severe and bloody consequences. In any other case, he would have been filled with fear and anxiety, but this was different; he was doing this for *Baldur,* his precious son.

He made his way silently down to where the ground opened up and the damp, musty smell of death wafted up into the skies. Patting his steed and comforting her, he sneaked down to the entrance, and with one last glance at the stairs, he descended into hell.

In his disguise, there was not a soul who could recognize him for the god, *Odin*, even those who knew him well. The more he searched, the more comfortable he became traversing through the depths of hell. That is, until he came to a magnificent hall adorned with elegant silks and endless tables of food and drink. It was not how he had envisioned the halls of the underworld, but it could all be a tool of deceit to draw him in and never release his soul to the world above again.

As curious as he was about the feast he had discovered, he still needed to find the seeress that could answer his burning question. Somewhere above him was his son, *Baldur*, who was completely unaware that his life could be in danger. It was all up to *Odin*, and so with new haste in his pace he continued his search.

When the seeress eventually revealed herself to *Odin*, he was immediately relieved because she spoke to him plainly, meaning she potentially did not suspect who he truly was. She had no reverence or fear in her sightless eyes, nor did she move to alert anyone, she simply spoke to him as if he was another wandering soul in the depths. He saw an opportunity to bond with the seeress and then hoped to find an opportunity to weave in his queries for his son's destiny.

"What a wondrous feast I came across on my way here. What could it be for?" He saw her raise an eyebrow in a moment of skepticism, but then she figured amongst the countless souls in the underworld, not all was included in the goings on of the grand halls.

"A feast indeed, meant for a god!" She cackled, her voice brittle like mud that had dried and cracked in the sun, "And indeed a god shall be the guest of honor!"

"What god is this?" *Odin* fought back the emotions that threatened to spill from his chest. He had to be a simple soul in hell, not a god seeking information on his son's fate.

"What other god would garner all this worship? Did you not see the food and the opulence? This is not an ordinary feast, nor will it be an ordinary night when it happens. You see, a mighty one shall fall soon. I have seen it." She tapped the side of her head and gave a strange, bent smile, proud of her inner sight.

"Such a god must be revered above all. Surely it is not *Odin* himself?"

She burst into a phlegm-filled laugh that caught in her throat several times. The seeress had found this quite amusing, as though it was intended as a joke.

"That end is not to come for a while yet, for Ragnarök is not yet upon us." She paused and cocked her head to one side, sniffing the air with her eyebrow raised again, but she continued on, "This feast is for *Baldur*, the beloved of all the gods. Surely, he is worthy of such a grand event if anyone is."

Odin felt his heart tear in two within his chest and he couldn't stop a wail from pouring forth from his mouth. He felt tears, hot and biting, stinging his eyes as he glared at the blind seeress who, despite being unable to see him, was wide-eyed and stiff. She suspected something was wrong about this imposter.

"You are no soul, nor do you belong here!" She raised a bony finger and pointed it towards his direction, "Who dares roam the halls of the underworld so boldly that none was the wiser?"

"You are right, seeress, I am no mere soul, nor is my hearth here in hell," he put off all disguise in his voice and let the deep, rumbling tone come out fully, "I am *Odin*, chieftain of the gods and creator of worlds. I am here for the answer you just provided, for I have dreamed of my son, *Baldur*, dying over and over. I was sure it was a prophecy, and you confirmed my worst fear, that my son would indeed die. But how, seeress, how?" He sobbed as he begged, though she knew full well that just because it was the underworld, it did not mean his power was any less. With a single thought, he could disembowel her, then repair her guts and do it all over again. She had heard the tales of his past, and so without hesitation, she answered.

"Deceit shall end your son's life. Lies from one that should not be trusted. Let nothing slip past, for that is when it all comes to a bloody end."

As he trudged out of the halls, he could hear her grating, cackling laughter echoing from pillar to pillar, following him until he finally emerged from the underworld and mounted back onto *Sleipnir*. *Odin* spurred her on to speeds she had never found before, all the while he was willing her to go faster. He would not lose his son, not to prophesy or any other magic out there. He was *Odin*, and he would not let it happen.

"There is no doubt left in my mind, for the seeress spoke the words I had feared," *Odin* was addressing the closest of his kin, *Frigg* by his side. He had gathered them the moment he discovered *Baldur* alive and well, but he knew that there was no assurance on how long it would be until this murder of deceit would come to pass, "This cannot be left to chance, nor to our will. It must be more than that. It must be iron clad that he is protected."

"Gather oaths!" *Frigg's* voice carried around the entire room like a forceful wind. She rarely spoke in these meetings, though her presence was always felt. Her eyes were red from crying, but her jaw was firm and set. "Gather oaths from every single one or thing that could cause him harm. If there is a chance that something could hurt *Baldur*, they shall give us their oath that nothing whatsoever shall happen—*ever*."

All around the room came solemn nods of agreement. Over the years *Odin* had gained the respect of all the gods, so as *Frigg* went to each one, they gave their oaths freely. There was not a single deity or object in existence that hesitated for even a moment, and so it was that *Frigg* returned home and presented *Odin* with an oath from each of the gods and from anyone who could hurt him. They embraced each other and then called their son to them; it was time he knew of the prophecy, now that there was nothing that could befall him.

It had been weeks since *Frigg* had collected the vows, and what was once a serious affair was now a fun game amongst the gods. Because *Baldur* was protected from all harm thanks to the oaths, there was nothing that could even bring on a bruise. It began when he was walking through a large room amongst other gods and, because of drink and clumsiness, a statue was bumped over into *Baldur*. Instead of catching it, the statue simply bounced off a field of protection around the god. The oaths had done their work, for nothing could come close to him let alone hurt him.

Ever since then, the gods had a ball of a time throwing sticks, rocks, and anything else available at *Baldur* just to watch them bounce off without him feeling a thing. Blades, fire, it made no difference; he was completely protected from everything and anything that could touch him. Or at least, that is what everyone thought.

There was only one thing in existence that had not sworn an oath to *Frigg*; the mistletoe. Of all things in the world, the goddess saw mistletoe as peaceful, calm, and of no threat to anyone. Because of this, she thought nothing of leaving it out of the oaths, however she kept that to herself. She knew how *Odin* worried, so she saw no benefit in telling him something in which there was no harm. In fact, she had completely forgotten about this until one rather common day.

On that day, she was sitting outside in the sun watching the birds flutter about when a handsome stranger wandered in and sat beside her.

She didn't know him, but somehow, she felt at ease beside him and saw no reason to be on her guard.

"Such a perfect day. Thanks be to *Odin*." The man said, smiling into the sky.

"Indeed, I am told he had a hand in it." They shared a small laugh together and suddenly it was like they were old friends. For hours they talked and shared stories, but then the stranger asked a rather odd question, not that *Frigg* noticed, as comfortable as she had become with the man.

"Such a stressful event, gathering all those oaths as you did," He gave a supportive smile and nod towards her as though he was congratulating her for her efforts, "I was curious, though, was there even one thing that did not take part in? For I heard that there was not one piece of existence missed, which is quite an undertaking."

For a moment she was going to hesitate and change the subject, but everything about the last few hours told her that this was a safe space and she could finally vent a secret she had not enjoyed keeping from *Odin*. Surely there was no harm in this, just two friends chatting without a purpose or agenda. Convinced that this stranger posed no harm or threat, she answered him honestly.

"To everyone else, there was not a thing missed, but between the two of us—if I may—there was *one* that I did not receive an oath from, though that was because I did not see the need. Of all things in all the worlds, the mistletoe has to be the least violent and least threatening of them all. I would sooner accuse a butterfly of murder than assume the mistletoe had malicious intent."

This seemed to satiate the stranger's curiosity as he changed the subject quickly. After another hour, he excused himself and left the courtyard, whistling to himself as he did. *Frigg* felt lighter than she had in weeks, all thanks to the kindness of a stranger and his conversation.

What she didn't know is that as the man turned the corner and hid in the shadows, he threw off a disguise to reveal *Loki*, the trickster, underneath. Of all the beings in the world, the last one who should have been trusted with such damning information as *Frigg* freely gave was *Loki*. No part of his mind wasn't slanted towards lies or chaos, all at the expense of as many as he could manage. It didn't take him long to put together a horrible plan for how he could use this new information in one of his many schemes. He had sensed that something was awry, but this was better than he could have ever expected.

He was never fond of the gods, let alone *Odin*, for the creator god always seemed to look down on the trickster, no matter how creative his actions were. For years, he had tried to express his usefulness, but it was as though *Odin* looked right through him unless there was a reason to yell or scold. It was finally his turn to grasp some control, and it was going to be directed fully at the one target that could cause chaos and pain to as many people as possible—he was going to kill *Baldur*. Well, to be more specific, he was going to make someone else kill *Baldur*, but his fingerprints were all over the intention.

For all the deception and trickery that was currently surrounding the mistletoe, the innocent plant had no clue about any of it. Content to remain quiet and focused on growing and existing; outside of that, there wasn't much in the world that seemed of any interest to it. The years passed, ages came and went, but the mistletoe simply *was* and would have been perfectly fine with that same status quo being kept for all eternity. Indeed, the span of time would have been much less bloody if the mistletoe had indeed remained offstage of the play of history. Unfortunately, that is not how it unfolded.

For a being as dubious and conniving as *Loki*, it did not take him long at all to find the mistletoe and if he had considered this a difficult task; he was suddenly much calmer than he had been before. Of all the things that exist in the world, there are those that desire power and others who desire peace, but there are few who have no qualms or desires to claim or desire anything other than to just *be*, and that is precisely how the mistletoe had lived its entire life. *Loki* had expected there to be a need for at least a modicum of craftiness, and yet he found himself able to walk right up to it with no sign that the mistletoe had noticed, or that it simply didn't care at all.

"Er, hello?" *Loki* really wasn't sure how to approach this situation since it was not at all what he had planned for. Until now it had been all disguises and creeping about, but suddenly he found himself directly in front of the one thing he needed for this entire plan to work out in his favor and he was feeling something he was not used to in any way at all; *Loki* was nervous.

He had gotten no response from the mistletoe, so he decided maybe it didn't hear him. The last thing he wanted was for him to snatch a few branches, and the startled plant would go into hysterics and alert anyone and everyone who was in range. It wouldn't take anyone long to see *Loki* looking guilty and cunning—as per usual—and assume he was up to no good. This had to be conducted with the only two participants being him and the mistletoe, which meant he needed to ensure a gentle touch.

"I say, this will never do," *Loki* said as he shook his head, arms folded, looking all around the base of the mistletoe. A few *tsk tsk*'s and he suddenly heard a very calm, very low voice respond.

"What's that, then? What will never do?"

"A thing as fine as yourself should never be in such a state!" He ruffled a few of the mistletoe's leaves and motioned about in a few general areas. In truth, there was nothing at all about the plant's appearance that needed addressing, but even the calmest of creatures had a streak of vanity—no matter how deep it was hidden. It was not the plan he thought he would end up using, but the moment he heard the concern in the tone of the response he knew that this was the right direction to go.

"Unkempt is all. I mean, I suppose if it doesn't bother *you*, it shouldn't be an issue. I was just thinking of what those passing by might think. However, as I said, if it doesn't bother *you*…" and *Loki* let his voice trail off. The most important thing to do now was to stay silent and let those words really sink in. It didn't take long before that calm, low voice spoke again.

"I do appreciate the concern," The mistletoe said, pausing for a moment as if it was trying to remember a name, but then continued on, "I admit I cannot tell where this unkempt section is, but as much as it humbles me to say I would like for those passing to admire and not look upon me with the concern I hear in your voice, traveler."

"It would take me not even a moment to fix this up," *Loki* cheerfully stated, motioning again in general to the base of the plant, "Then you will have everyone who passes by looking on and smiling."

The response was more of a sound than a word, but *Loki* knew the noise of approval when it was made. For all the trickery he excelled at, in this particular case, there was an air of truth to what he had promised. In some other life perhaps, *Loki* would have made a wonderful gardener or a florist on some London corner shop, for he could have simply grabbed a few branches and been on his way but for some reason— probably even unknown to *Loki* himself when he left, branches in hand—he did so with the mistletoe looking more trimmed and tidier than it had in years.

Granted, it was hardly a trade-off for the horrific reason he needed the branches in the first place, but a moment of compassion in the midst of deception is like seeing a flower in a desert; beautiful but sad because of its surroundings. The brief moment that showed the existence of a heart had no impact on the actions that followed, for if the mistletoe had known what those branches would be used for no amount of charm or sweet tones would have convinced it to go along.

The game of throwing anything and everything at Baldur to watch them fall harmlessly to the side was still going on when *Loki* sneaked back into the midst of the very beings he despised. Laughter and drink were plentiful, but he was only interested in one of the gods; *Hodr*. If the moment of empathy earlier impacted *Loki,* it was long gone by the time he finally laid eyes on the god he was searching for.

Of all the gods who were standing about throwing their weapons and stones at Baldur, there was only one who was not eagerly taking part, but it was not because of a lack of desire. You see, for all the power held within his form, the god *Hodr* was completely blind. While that did not allow the god to enjoy himself with his other immortal peers, it did mean that he was the perfect target for what *Loki* had planned.

The energy was chaotic as the gods took turns choosing weapons or various items and launching them directly at Baldur, each one falling harmlessly to the side while Odin's son simply smiled and winked at whoever threw it. In the beginning, it had been scary and strange, but as more and more things were tossed and not a single one got near him, his confidence was at an all-time high. He even began taunting different gods and hinting at which weapons would be the most impressive to be thrown, each time with a laugh that echoed in the chamber.

All of this was to *Loki*'s advantage because had most taken notice of him, they would have kept a sharp eye on wherever he was. Almost every pair of seeing eyes were aimed directly at the center of the room where the protected god was still openly encouraging the surrounding crowd, now fully embracing being the center of attention. This left *Loki*'s eyes and the sightless eyes of *Hodr* as the only ones not involved in the happenings of the moment.

"Pity," *Loki* said, disguising his voice slightly, although in the din of the room the tone of his voice was barely audible, so the words themselves were what truly mattered. No response from the blind god. Moving closer to *Hodr* and placing a hand on the god's shoulder, *Loki* got right down near his ear and continued, ensuring that they were the only two privy to the conversation.

"Truly a pity," This time *Loki knew Hodr had* heard, for swiftly came the melodious words of *Hodr* that everyone assumed was the exchange for his sight; a wondrous voice for his eyes. However, it had occurred, it had brought him to this place where he assumed he was speaking to a well-meaning member of the *Aesir*, unaware that the trickster himself was laying a trap of sorrow and tears that was falling into place rather perfectly.

"What is this pity you speak of?" *Hodr* answered, perplexed by the words this stranger spoke, for all he heard about him was joy and celebration.

"I simply speak of all this glee and happiness being had by all, and yet the wondrous god, *Hodr*, sits alone without the means to participate himself. It is a pity, indeed, that no one has offered a single morsel of assistance. They are all too concerned with enjoying the time themselves. Where does that leave you, great *Hodr*?" *Loki* let the question hang in the air, waiting for *Hodr* to pick up on the direction he was leading.

"It leaves me here."

"And are you enjoying yourself?"

"The pleasure of my fellow gods is enough—"

"That is not what I asked, for of course, a being as compassionate and kind as you would want to take joy in the joy of others. Does it not matter that *you* are being denied that joy, though? That in a room full of those who call themselves your kin, none have attempted to bring you into the fold of the celebration?"

Hodr didn't respond to this one, he simply remained facing forward, towards where most of the noise was coming from. It seemed that as *Loki* finished talking, the voices of the gods actually became louder and the laughter more pronounced. Each passing second seemed to make *Hodr* more and more tense until he let out a huff and turned his head to where *Loki* was hunched over.

"Is your intent to bring this up to shame me?"

"Never!" *Loki* feigned being aghast at this accusation, when in fact that was the precise purpose of every word he had said to the god, "I tell you all this because while the gods around you may not care if you take part as well, I do care."

"Oh?" *Hodr* cocked his head, showing that his interest had been piqued. "And you can do something about this, can you?" It was the exact thing *Loki* had been navigating the conversation towards. He had his opening and everything was in place for him to take advantage of it.

"I would never speak of such things without being able to offer not only assistance, but the means with which to experience the same joy you hear all around you." And with those words, *Loki* took a smooth, sharp spear from under his cloak; the one he had whittled and sharpened from the branches of the mistletoe plant. Without a word, he led *Hodr's* hand to the base of the spear and *Loki*'s eyes gleamed with an evil sheen as he saw *Hodr* smile at the touch of the weapon.

"Well, isn't this a wondrous thing to appear? I feel the weight of a well-made spear. Oh friend, why bring it for this use?" *Hodr* apparently was still slightly unsure about why all this was happening, but *Loki* could see that it would only take a few more moments for him to be fully convinced. He hadn't come this far just to fail and be forced to watch yet another win for the gods; it was time for *Loki* to get his turn.

"Only the fates know that answer, for I felt the urge to bring it with me this day and it was the same feeling that brought me to your side. Some things in this life go to extreme lengths to seek their purpose, and it seems that you finding this spear was the purpose all along," *Loki* smiled and put his hands on the shoulders of the god, "How does it feel in your hands? A magnificent weapon for a magnificent being."

That was the moment that shifted it all, for it had been far too long since someone had given him such praise. He was a god, that is true, and a glory-filled member of the *Aesir*, but there was a clear difference between the gods that were paid attention to and praised on a daily—sometimes hourly—basis simply for being who they were. While they were having laud heaped upon them, where was he? Always there, but hardly noticed.

"Come closer, friend," *Hodr* whispered, tugging lightly at the robe around *Loki*'s neck. Quick to stop his cowl from slipping and letting his face be revealed to all, he bent down and placed his ear as close to the aged lips of the god as he could without having flesh on flesh.

"Speak what you will, mighty *Hodr*, for I am honored to listen." *Loki* already had the blind *Aesir* lounging in the palm of his hand, but the trickster was ever greedy and that one extra step always had to be taken otherwise what was the fun of it at all? For every moment that he could devote to stroking the oft-ignored ego of *Hodr*, it was another inch deeper that metaphorical dagger would slide into the backs of every single god in the room, as well as all who would hear the echo of the deed *Loki* was creeping towards.

"My pride urges me to toss this weapon without care; whispering that I cannot possibly miss. However, my humility that has grown with the passing of time has a louder voice that reminds me of my age, my weakened state, and that what little confidence and sense of self I have left would be put to ruin if I were to embarrass myself.

"For all my griping and mumbling, the opinion of those around both you and I have much more of an impact on my spirit than I would ever readily admit to. However, with your kind touch, this gift of more than a tool, more than a spear, and more than a weapon—the gift of a *moment* regained—and an opportunity that rarely presents itself to men like me anymore, even here in *Asgard*.

"For all my anticipation, however, I must beg of you one single task that will enable me to gladly and willingly accept this offering of monumental importance to my heart and soul," *Hodr* paused a moment and with a deep breath he lifted his hand so that *Loki* could look directly upon it, and what he saw were the tremors of the mind slowly unraveling itself from the body."

Sight was not the only thing that was bringing the god the inner pain he felt each day, even a god felt his age from time to time and for *Hodr* that time was becoming more and more consistent, "You must guide my hand so that my strike flies true and instead of shame, I shall join in the frivolity and kinship that is being shared all over this room. Can you do this for me?"

"Again, you show me honor with this request," *Loki* let his voice drip with emotion, playing his part so well that he was almost drooling with the gleeful desire to see it all come to fruition, "Give me your hand and I shall give you a gentle touch to signal when you should throw the magnificent weapon in your grasp."

A smile that had barely touched *Hodr's* face for years was now a permanent fixture, or so the glow from the joy felt by the god seemed to display. It took *Loki* no more than a few moments to ensure that *Hodr* was holding onto the spear with a tight grip, and with a few checks down the shaft to avoid missing the target—or else all the effort would be for nothing—*Loki* inhaled and tasted the sweet revenge he had been dreaming of ever since the first time one of the *Aesir* looked down their noses at him.

As the universe floats through existence, weaving in and out of time, there are a few moments that resound from the outer edge of the darkness to the revolving planets that make up our galaxy. These moments are so significant that they bring everything to a brief pause almost as if the complex, moving parts that make up the universe were shocked and stunned to the extent that the massive momentum of existence slowed to watch it go by.

Of all the moments that had come before, this was the one that would be remembered as the catalyst for the end. As the surrounding events began to build to the action itself, it was as though the fates themselves were holding their collective breath in anticipation of something so powerful and jarring that it triggered prophecy to come true.

Whether *Loki* was aware of the depth that his actions would reach or not had little sway over the matter because it all seemed to be set up for precisely the right moment—*the* moment—to occur. With the breath of fate and the universe held as one, *Loki* smiled and released chaos.

Hodr felt the rough bark that stood out against the smoother parts of the shaft as it came to the point; sharp and sheer as a spear ever was. It had been ages since he had felt the life spark in his blood, and as he gripped the weapon tighter in his hand, he could feel his skin prickle and the hair on his neck stood on edge. With a slow inhale, he steadied himself and gave *Loki* the silent signal that all was ready for *Hodr* to have his moment in the sun. He might not realize, but he was trembling inside in anticipation of the acceptance that would finally recognize him again. It was *Hodr's* time now, and every thought in his mind was wild, and more alive than he had felt in far too long.

For all his fear that time would have caused his skills to rust, he had no issue recalling the movement and thrust needed to propel a weapon of death through the air. It might not have been the same as how it felt in the red-hot surge of battle, but as it left *Hodr's* hand he couldn't help but feel a swell of pride in anticipation of the glory that attention would surely bring.

He waited for a moment following the throw, but there was no one patting him on the back or even a shout of congratulations; all that came after the sound of the spear cutting through the air was quite the opposite of what he had expected. It wasn't just that no one was celebrating. There was a distinct absence of frivolity and the jovial nature that had filled the space not seconds before. A few moments later *Hodr* would dream of that silence as if it was the best thing he would ever experience, because the wails echoed off every wall and surface. The core-scraping, blood-boiling cries of beings who were not used to seeing what they had just witnessed.

Hodr had envisioned the shaft bouncing harmlessly to the side in the same way it had been described by the cheers and shouting—perhaps, at absolute best, *Baldur* would reach out and catch it. What an honor that would have been, but it was not what happened. Not at all what happened.

Every other piece of weaponry, shrapnel, and some of the more creative *Aesir* sections of the furniture had been blessed by the promise of peace that *Frigg* had sought from what all had assumed was everything in creation. What *Hodr* had thrown, however, was the keystone in *Loki*'s underhanded plot. The sharp point of the mistletoe burst through the protection and struck the god in the heart, passing through his body, and fell with a clatter in an ever-growing pool of the most sacred blood to spill on those stones.

Baldur, beloved of all the gods, could only look down at the hole in his chest and gape at those around him as he fell forward, both hands clawing the ground in an effort to reach a cure that was nowhere to be found. After a few moments of futile screams and shocked mutterings, the final fragments of life drained from the body of *Baldur* and all that was left were his eyes—surprised, hurt, and lifeless—and the one, still, reaching hand that was stretched out towards the most unlikely of suspects; *Hodr*.

The only two who knew how the mistletoe had been left off her list never spoke a word of it, save for the conversation one had with the other—*Frigg* was now pale as a sheet, her eyes filling with white-hot tears and her throat unable to produce sound, but where was *Loki*?

"What has happened?" *Hodr* whispered, not even sure he wanted to hear the response but had a horrible, sinking feeling when no answer came at all. He tried again, "Friend, what has caused this inverse of sound that has collapsed into my ears? For all my senses I cannot make up for what my eyes would have seen—be my eyes again."

"*Hodr*," came a voice from across the room. It was tight with emotion yet firm with some inner choice to not let it out. "*Hodr*, you speak to no one." *Odin* could only get those words out, and what he said was true. *Loki*, the hooded stranger, and provider of *Hodr*'s death, bringing a weapon, was nowhere to be seen, and because of the chaos that had been joyfully erupting only a few short minutes earlier, no one else had seen anyone who would have fit that description. All they knew was that somehow *Hodr* had gotten through the assumed protection; the details didn't seem all that important in the moment.

Frigg knew she had to regain control over this situation because it wouldn't take long for the magic among those in the chamber to somehow discern where this all began. She had the image of the stranger in the courtyard swirling in her mind, and she just *knew* it had to be the same one that deceived poor, harmless *Hodr* into slaying such a beauteous thing as *Baldur* was.

"There is no time to waste staggering about like a party of mourners," she exclaimed, her hands held aloft for all to see. *Odin* was still letting the truth of reality permeate the thick shell of shock, so she spoke for them both.

"The very soul of our beloved son, *Baldur*, hangs in the balance. Who shall ride to the very depths, into the fire, and retrieve that which can make him whole again? Who shall dare defy the rights to death for me? For *Odin*? For us all?"

In her mind, she had the fleeting thought to shift any hint of blame onto the one who actually *threw* the spear, but there was enough that could go against her and the scales of her heart were leaning greatly towards an evil place. She needed this to be about heroism and revenge against something bigger than one target—this was a ride against death itself, if she could will it to become so.

Youth breeds bravery, but youth rarely faces that which would *grow* the courage needed to not just ride into glory, but return as well. One of those who had few years on his face was *Hermod*, one of the more forgotten sons of *Odin*, but it still mattered in his heart. Hearing the call to be the hero, *Hermod* always dreamed of his father recognizing him and before he knew it, he was being readied in the saddle of *Odin*'s own steed, *Sleipnir*, with instructions to ride straight into the deepest parts of *Hel* and do whatever was needed to bring *Baldur* back to where he belonged; back to *Asgard*.

Off rode *Hermod*, his head full of the cheers he was certain would greet him upon his triumphant return, but whether he ever made it back or not—in truth, even if Frigg never got her *Baldur* back—her secret would remain such. What she needed to do right away was to ensure that his burial would be something that all would remember; the kind of ceremony that consumed legend and gave birth to mythical tales. That was *one* thing she needed, but what she truly desired was something she could never speak aloud; not a mention or whisper, for even that risked it falling on *any* ears. It was one of those thoughts that lurk near the bottom of the mind, never daring to venture near the surface but still real and alive—more than that, though, it was *true*.

Frigg felt like she had been living in a minefield ever since she realized her responsibility for the death of *Baldur*. It seemed like every move brought with it an intricate dance around the armed and hidden explosives, just waiting to destroy her world in one fiery moment. There had been more than a few moments when she was *sure* that her secret was about to become public knowledge, and yet she emerged from each inferno without a single burn—at least that others could see. Underneath that unscathed exterior was a weary, guilt-ridden, paranoid woman.

Hermod was used to moving fast. Of all his brothers and peers, he was always the one who finished first in their races, even when he didn't try as hard as the others. This kind of speed was something else entirely, though. *Sleipnir* didn't just gallop, he practically flew as they sped by villages and mountains, leaping effortlessly over rivers and at one point skimming gracefully across the surface of a lake. Despite the grim nature of his quest, *Hermod* couldn't help but find himself smiling as he clung to the steed, the wind whipping past as they continued towards their final destination.

When *Hermod* first set out, he had expected this ride to take quite some time, and he had prepared himself for weeks of riding and time to consider how he would go about convincing the goddess of Hel herself to release a soul; and not just *any* soul, one that was surely among the rarest in her collection.

After the first few days passed, though, he realized that there was fast, then *Hermod* fast, but riding this spectacular beast was a pace he had never gotten close to reaching—this would not be the lengthy ride he had expected.

While there were certainly positives to be found in that fact—the main one being that if he *was* successful, his news would return with him much faster than previously anticipated—but as he watched yet another blur of landscape go by he was focused on one matter; he now had much, *much* less time with which to come up with a plan. If there had been a party with him, then he would have held back his emotions and hidden the fear, but it was just him and the horse, so he began to weep openly. It wasn't the tears of someone who had given up or believed that this would only end in failure; it was the reaction to immense pressure suddenly becoming *very* real.

It had been pure bravado that made him volunteer himself for this mission, and while he didn't regret it, he wished that there had been even a semblance of a plan before he put himself in this position. Bravado could get you so far, but when it came down to actually fulfilling the purpose for this entire endeavor, he would need something much more reliable than a confident whim. The more he thought about it, the more he began to realize how utterly unprepared he was for this on so many different levels.

It wasn't that he was helpless or without strengths, but if you had taken him and placed the young god beside the other *Aesir* who had also been struck deep by *Baldur's* death, *Hermod* would not have been the first choice for a task as crucial as this. In fact, if he was being painfully honest with himself, he wouldn't have been in the top ten, let alone the one who was chosen to go forth as he had done.

It was *much* too late for these kinds of second-guessing thoughts to be invading his psyche, but he supposed it was better to struggle with all of this *now* rather than when he was actually at the gates of Hel itself.

It had been six days, and the environments hadn't changed all that much until the last hour or so, which brought a chill that *Hermod* was not at all fond of. Much to his frustration and discomfort, the chill quickly became a snow flurry, but thankfully that was the extent of the colder weather that they faced. Perhaps it was the tremendous speeds they were going at, but even with the unfortunate cold spot and the snow that he *truly* could have done without, he saw something in the distance that was quite different from anything in their journey so far.

The sky wasn't its usual blue, or even a darker shade as the night beckoned; a reddish hue gripped the sky, and not the kind one would expect from a sunset or foreboding of a storm—this was almost *unnatural.* The closer they got, the more he could see beneath the red, overhanging atmosphere on the horizon, and it seemed like what he was seeing was more a symptom than the disease. In other words, it wasn't the red clouds he should be focused on; it was the gaping cave leading down to Hell that the scarlet mist in the air was circling.

It was the first time since they had set out that *Sleipnir* slowed his pace whatsoever, and the drastic change in speeds made the distance to the cavern seem like an eternity. It was a mournful moment, but he suddenly realized that he had been given a gift when all seemed quite hopeless, or at least improbable at best; he now had *time*!

Whether *Odin's* mighty steed that had carried *Hermod* across sensed his rider's need for some extra time or not, the comparison between the speed they *were* going at and what *Sleipnir* had slowed to create a massive gap rather than a mere difference.

For the first few minutes, all that could be heard was the out-loud musings of *Hermod* on just exactly how he was planning on actually *doing* the thing he had set out do to. He hadn't volunteered to ride all the way here and then turn around, after all, so he was determined to walk down that path to Hel with a plan of some kind; it might not be the best plan, or even one of the better ones, but having one at all was at least something.

"Hello," He began as he went through another scenario, trying to imagine what he may encounter below the surface. He stopped himself short the moment he began speaking and shook his head in disgust. "*Hello?* That is how I am going to greet the ruler of Hel, the daughter of *Loki?* I mean, this is *Hel* herself that I will be speaking to, so it had better be something more impactful than *Hello*."

He went round and round with himself, thinking of different ways to approach it, but each time he ended up feeling like a fool and he was certain that a fool stood *very* little chance against *Hel. Hermod* was still going through scenarios in his mind when he noticed they weren't just moving slowly. They had stopped.

With a slow, unwilling motion, he looked up and saw that they were, in fact, staring directly into the mouth of a gigantic cave. The red sky above was shadowy and flashes of blue and green lightning filled the sky with colored bursts, yet they were anything but cheerful. The glow cast an eerie light on the entrance to *Hel*—or at least the first step to getting there—and it certainly didn't make *Hermod* any more eager to begin making his descent.

"I may not know what I am doing, but this isn't about me," He said to himself, gathering every single bit of confidence and strength he could within himself, "This is about *Baldur*, and *Hodr*, and *Frigg*, and *Odin*; this is for the lost, and those who lost them. I will not waver, and it isn't because I have no fear—it is because my love for them is stronger than anything I might be frightened of!"

With those words and a gentle nudge to let *Sleipnir know now he was* ready, they began the slow and steady way downwards into *Hel*.

It had been too long since *Hermod* rode to the world of the dead to retrieve the soul of *Baldur*, and with each passing day *Odin* became less and less the husband *Frigg* knew and more like the empty, stoic form wearing the face of the chief *Aesir*. He hadn't slept, not that she had seen, and all his time had been spent either standing at the edge of the water or watching from the balcony of their bedroom for any sign that *Hermod* had returned with any news at all.

Frigg would wake, wonder for a brief moment if everything had been a dream, and then she would see *Odin* standing in the same position; both hands planted firmly on the railing as he surveyed the horizon, the gates of *Asgard* so that he wouldn't miss the first sign of news.

On the ninth day she finally decided to see if she had been wrong in giving her husband space, and instead required a more direct approach to snap him from this endless cycle of depression.

"Still nothing, my love?" She asked, her hands resting on his shoulders, trying to show comfort without overdoing it. He had never been like this before, and she was doing everything in her power to not show how much it was frightening her. She knew well that the full brunt of his power would be a terrible force indeed, and if circumstances didn't somehow improve, she could see him burn it all to ash and then turn to the other worlds as well. She had quietly been trying to discover where *Loki* had taken himself to, but considering the victory he had just achieved, it was hardly a surprise that he had not been heard from or seen.

"I keep looking." Then he paused for much longer than she knew what to do with. It seemed to go on for ages as his mouth hung partly agape and his eyes never left the edge of the sky. She wanted to cough or touch his arm; anything that would remind him to continue, but she gave him this pause to see where it took them. "I keep looking for anything to show that *Herm*–that he was back. Hours on end I am vigilant, but the sun sets, and I am left in the darkness–" he stopped short, his voice wavering as his shoulders began to shake, "The same darkness that my boy is in now, and the same one my other boy has gone off to. Both sent to the chasm of black and silent pain. For what? A chance? I can feel it in the center of myself, *Frigg*, and it doesn't feel like this will be a victory for us."

"And what does a victory look like? A victory for us, as you say?" She wanted him to focus on something positive, and even if it had to be the practically impossible future where everything worked out, she would use it to try to bring him back from whatever ledge he had been perched at since *Baldur* was struck down.

It had been less than a week and already the impact that was felt from *Baldur's* absence was being felt across the vast worlds that *Odin* had built. The skies seemed darker even when it was day and the clouds almost loomed instead of floated above the ground. The winds were never calm and breezy, but whipped and howled as if it too was feeling the sorrow that enveloped all of *Asgard*. *Odin* lifted his head towards *Frigg* and was about to answer when he stood up suddenly, his eyes alight, and the closest thing his face could do to a smile appeared. He turned to his wife and grabbed her shoulders, looking her straight in the eyes.

"Was that a trumpet?"

"Was what—"

"Was that a trumpet, woman?" He roared, yet somehow his tone remained hopeful even at that aggressive volume. She hesitated because she didn't know if this was the last piece of his sanity falling away, but then he turned and dashed off through the bedroom and out the door before she could respond. Then she heard it too; it was definitely a trumpet—and somehow even that sounded sad.

Odin barely felt his feet touch any of the stairs or hallways that he raced down on his way to where he had heard the trumpet signal from. Considering the damper that the recent events had brought to *Asgard*, hearing any sound other than rain and the wind was strange indeed, but it also meant that *Odin* knew exactly where it had come from—where the Rainbow Bridge entered this world, and where *Hermod* would ride in from.

The head of the *Aesir* allowed himself to get his hopes higher than ever before because the only alternative was the end of all things and he couldn't let himself accept that as a reality. The trumpet sounded again and this time *Odin* was close enough to see the trumpeter and the reason for the multiple signals; *Hermod* had indeed returned.

With a pace rapid in nature yet anxious in energy, *Odin* was halfway to where his son's horse was standing before he caught the look on his face and there was no need to ask the only question on his mind. It was hard to mistake the expression of total devastation mixed with absolute shock, and *Hermod's* face was covered in both to a powerful and worrying extreme. It was the look of a man who had come face to face with his own insufficiencies and would probably hold that image in his mind for the rest of his days.

He felt like he had returned and brought darkness with him; utter black except where one glimmer of hope remained, but even that was too small for him to place hope in, especially after what he had witnessed in Hel. No matter what anyone could ever say to him, *Hermod* knew the unbiased truth—he would always see this result as his failure.

This one chance—the only chance he had ever had and the only one he would ever see—had ended in complete and utter failure, and what was worse is he didn't know the full extent of what it meant. He knew Odin had been broken in two—as was still confirmed when he saw his father's face—but this seemed bigger and more important than a father wanting to rescue his favorite son; there was no delusion in *Hermod's* mind, and he had long made his peace with it, but it still didn't mean this level of ruin that had fallen onto his father was a relevant response to what had happened.

"My son."

"Father," *Hermod* nearly whispered this as he respectfully kissed *Odin* in greeting.

"Am I to glean from your expression that you truly return empty-handed?"

"I may not have returned with my brother, as you would have desired, but that does *not* mean I have come back with nothing at all."

Odin paused, because this was something he did not expect. All the days of watching for *Hermod* without success had brought every dark thought in his mind to the surface. It had been days of pain and silent suffering, but for the first time in what seemed like centuries, *Odin* felt a glimmer of hope from what his son had said.

"Explain yourself." *Odin* didn't want riddles or stories. He wanted to know how this could all be undone. It had been a dream that diminished by the hour, but he felt himself believing again that it could be fixed—not just repaired, but returned to a place where it never happened.

"It is true that the guardian of the dead, *Hel*, did not want to give up the soul of *Baldur*, but after days of negotiation, she agreed to his release *if* we could provide her with something in return."

"*Hel* herself has asked something of us?" *Odin* felt his hope deflate. The soul of an *Aesir* was a valuable thing indeed, and *Hel* was not one to easily let a treasure like that slip from her grasp—be it *Odin's* son or not, "What task has she set before us?"

"Though I feared that all the speeches in the world wouldn't sway *Hel*, I had no other option at hand considering that I was in the depths— nay, the very heart—of her world, so it was no time for weapons to be drawn unless I wanted to hand over a second son of *Odin* to her clutches.

"So, I told her of *Baldur* and what he meant to those that had him taken from them. I wept and begged, letting her see the true level of pain and misery that this one death had caused. Without end, I went through the blessing he was to each being he encountered, and just when I was beginning to feel as though nothing would work, she saw the truth in my eyes. That is when she told me that it was all fine and good for me to *tell* her about how much he meant, but if I could get *every single thing* in existence to weep for the lost life of *Baldur*, then he would indeed be brought back from her realm and reunited in *Asgard* with his kin."

"Then that is what we shall do!" *Odin* was already hurrying back, shouting for *Frigg* to round up all the things in the world. He meant it too; *all* the things. Animals and people, trees, winds, and bodies of water they all were imbued with the spark of creation, and so each had a voice in the collection of worlds

Hermod was left standing beside his horse, feeling mildly happy for the hope he had given his father, but there had been a glint of laughter in *Hel's* eye when she made the deal. This was not what it appeared to be, and though in the moment the solution seemed to be there for the taking, he was sure this would not end in joy when the last word was said in the matter.

It was no exaggeration to say that *Baldur's* death was truly felt by all creatures in the world, for these were the very same who had made a solemn oath to keep him from harm before the betrayal of *Loki*. That is why it was easier than *Odin* expected to call all living things to *Asgard* so they could weep for the fallen *Baldur* and prove their sorrow to *Hel*, who would watch from the dim light of her world to ensure that not a single creature was missed or refused.

For such a monumental event with such high stakes, it only seemed right for all the *Aesir* to be present, so a feast was thrown in the large hall where a massive semi-circular table seated all the gods and each creature could enter and weep in the sight of all. One by one, they came in and each one wept mightily, none with a hint of falseness to their tears. The line wound around the forests, hills, and rivers for miles; every one of them eager to do their part for *Odin* and *Frigg*. Even the mistletoe, shamed by the part it had played despite the fault being with *Frigg* for that, entered and wept the loudest, wanting to make amends for all that had transpired.

Not one being that came into that hall did anything but weep and appease *Hel*, but considering the breadth of the task before *Odin,* there was still much to do before *Hel* would have seen what she needed to.

Finally, the line was nearing an end after weeks of watching one creature after another walk in, say a few kind words, and then weep for what they had lost in *Baldur.* A donkey, several horses, five birds, more than a few dwarves, an elf and his companion, and at the very end of the once immense line was a huge giantess named *Thokk,* who was slightly hunched with a black shawl around her shoulders.

Within an hour the elf entered the hall, companion in tow, leaving *Thokk* as the last one to be standing in wait for her turn. As the two—elf and company—left the hall and went on their way, red-eyed and still sniffling from the open expression they had shown, *Thokk* was led through the massive doorway made from incredibly large pieces of lumber and shown to the center point of the hall where the seated *Aesir* were waiting for this long journey to appease *Hel* to be complete. It was more than that, though—they wanted *Baldur* back, and it was so close that *Odin* could taste it.

Frigg could barely contain herself as she saw the last being in line come in, because that meant she was only one more weeping creature away from putting all this behind her; the anguish caused, the naivety, the mistakes would all be forgotten—or never known at all. The tension in the room could only be described as though the air itself decided to hold its breath, with the only sound coming from the muffled *thuds* of the giantess's feet hitting the ground with every step.

As *Thokk* cleared her throat to prepare for the short words of remembrance that preceded the tears there seemed to be something *very* familiar to *Frigg* about the shawl that the massive woman at the center of the room was wearing, but she couldn't put her finger on it and considering the moment it seemed silly to cling to that fleeting thought. Her inner process was interrupted by the deep, guttural voice of *Thokk* filling the room.

"It is truly unfortunate that I did not have the opportunity—no—*the honor* of knowing *Baldur* more than just in reputation and wonderful tales," A murmur of agreement swept through the chamber, with each seated *Aesir* nodding solemnly towards the giantess as she continued, "And it would be the greatest privilege I could ever expect to receive to be the final turn of the key that unlocks our beloved and now-lost *Baldur*," she paused again, but this time everyone felt the air change a bit as *Thokk* lifted her head and pulled the shawl closer around her shoulders before locking eyes with *Frigg*, who was still befuddled by this feeling that she had seen that wrap before.

Then, like fifty tons of rock, it struck her so hard that she felt the breath leave her body in a single gasp. Like a fish gasping on land, she opened and closed her mouth, a trembling hand trying to motion towards *Thokk,* but every part of her body was in shock and unable to perform the simplest of tasks. She knew! She remembered where she had seen the shawl before and it wasn't around the shoulders of a giantess. It had been around the shoulders of a kind stranger who had sat with her in a courtyard and talked of so many things for hours on end—it belonged to *Loki!*

"No," She tried to speak, to yell, but even the word she got out was barely audible, thankfully because of the respectful silence that was usually kept in this hall, her husband heard the sound and turned to his wife.

"Did you say something, my dearest?"

She would have done her best to answer him, but someone else beat her to the punch.

"She said *No.*"

Odin turned very slowly towards *Thokk* because though it was still a giantess before them, the voice was no longer the same as the one who had spoken earlier. He knew this voice, but could hardly believe that one could be so bold as to show up here, and today of all days. Then his heart fell as he realized the reason for this, but it was too late. He had let the one thing that could disrupt everything right into this very hall, as though he was serving the soul of *Baldur* on a silver platter.

"As I said, it *would* be my greatest privilege, but I cannot weep for *Baldur*, nor do I desire his soul and self returned to us. Let *Hel* have him, and may she enjoy it!"

Odin knew *Hel* had heard from her realm, and he also knew that with those words, it had truly come to an end. *Baldur* was gone and would remain so from now until the end of time. There was an angry uproar from all those in the room, but then they all gasped as one when *Thokk* began to convulse and moan, shaking in place while the air around her seemed to shimmer and distort. Then, in a sudden flash of light, it was no longer a giantess standing there, but a grinning, practically glowing *Loki.*

"You know, *Frigg*," the trickster said, looking right into her eyes, "I'm surprised that you seem so distraught at all this, considering your role."

"You have nothing but lies within you and so that is all that will spew forth!" *Frigg* screamed, wanting to drown out his words as he was inches from revealing it all to her husband and the rest of the *Aesir.*

"True, true," *Loki* nodded with false solemnity, "I am known for my lies, but then again, I may have some truths floating around in there that I feel are *very* interesting indeed. After all, someone had to miss it," he paused and a dark gleam entered his eyes, "Miss it, you know, miss the mistletoe. An oversight, of course, but still," he sucked air through his teeth and gave a few *tsks* in her direction.

"Everyone knows you were the one behind the death of our beloved *Baldur*! After the countless times you have brought pain and suffering upon those in this room, we hardly need proof to consider you guilty!" *Frigg* was on her feet, hands on the table before her, face flushed as she raged on. *Odin*, however, just sat there staring first at *Loki* and then at his wife with an expression that was a lovechild between hurt and the worst anger imaginable. Somehow *Frigg* knew deep down that she had lost it all, but she had to fight and believe that she could still fix this.

"That would fit with how I have been treated throughout my existence, but these next words are not for you, *Frigg*, they are for your mourning, certainly confused, husband," and *Loki* turned his eyes to focus on the head of the *Aesir* who was still seated and unable to fully react to anything going on around him, "*Odin*, haven't you asked yourself why, if your wife swore that she truly got *all* things to swear their oath, then why did a weapon crafted from the mistletoe—that she *missed*—find its way into the flesh of your late *Baldur*?"

These words were enough to bring *Odin* to his feet, and that in turn caused most of the *Aesir* to stand as well. The anger kept rising, the shouting began and echoed all around the room, while *Loki* stood in the midst of it, looking quite pleased with himself despite being surrounded by those who certainly wanted him dead. Then his face shifted from confident to terrified, just for a moment, but it was brought on by *Odin's* mighty yell.

"Someone find me *Thor*!"

Loki was reckless, impulsive, underhanded, and quite a few adjectives with rather negative definitions, but one thing he wasn't was naïve about what his brother would do when he found out the role he had played in *Baldur's* death. It was all fun and games when only the ones around the table were threatening, but now it had gotten serious and *Loki* had never been very good at serious.

It only took a brief moment for *Loki* to concentrate amongst the cacophony of shouting and shift himself into something that could get him out of here and keep going for a while. He knew how fast the *Aesir* were when they had a purpose, so *Thor* wouldn't be long in storming through the doorway. The angry crowd of gods was suddenly shocked and very confused as *Loki* was no longer standing in the center of the room, but an incredibly fast falcon was streaking through the doorway and out into the free air beyond the hall. It wasn't a moment too soon either, because right then *Thor* raced into the room, breathless, hammer held aloft, shouting the name of his brother. It only took him a second to take in the expressions and energy of the room to know that *Loki* had gotten away—again.

Upon hearing that, of all the *Aesir*, it was *Baldur* who was being laid to rest. There was not a single group without representation at the event; elves, dwarves, man and beast alike, winged and with hooves. If it drew breath of the usual kind or sparked with magic and myth, it was in the crowd that gathered at the water's gleaming edge. *Asgard*—though still a beacon of beauty and power—seemed to be dimmed as the gods themselves bowed their heads while *Odin* and *Frigg* walked down the procession line to where the massive, elegantly carved boat (named *Hringhorni* by *Baldur* himself) waited with the body of the dead god.

"We are here to lay to rest one who was not simply *our* son," *Frigg* touched her husband on the shoulder as she let her voice ring out to all that had gathered to pay their respects to the fallen *Aesir*, "For he was a son to us all!" A clamor of agreement swept through those in the crowd but then a terrible wail tore through the lowered sound as *Nanna*, the ever-loyal wife of *Baldur*, made her way, sobbing and staggering, as the crowds moved to the sides to let her through.

"My *Baldur*," her voice shook with the tremors of a shattered heart as she fell into the waiting arms of *Frigg*, who knew that after such a showing as this there would be no talk of a hunt of blame, so she held the new widow tight. With each renewed burst of tears, *Nanna* pulled against *Frigg* and tried to make her way onto the boat-turned-pyre where her husband was lying.

"No, no," soothed *Frigg*, holding her back, "Let him be. Now he rests."

With the sound of a sob being swallowed, *Nanna* did her best to hold the violent tears at bay. *Thor* came forward and as he held his mighty hammer over the pyre, a hallowed flame crept through the wood and engulfed the entire structure in a slow-burning, wondrous flame. It did not turn to ash, but rather burned bright without end as all had wished the heart of *Baldur* had done.

The solemnity of the moment covered the entire crowd as *Odin* went to push the boat out onto the waters. He did so without issue until the bottom struck a sandy outcrop and he had to use incredible effort to push it back onto its watery path, but then again, the rising and falling of the water's floor made it an arduous process. Then, from deep at the back of the masses, came a thundering voice, deep but not angry, as *Hyrrokkin*, greatest of the giantesses, came forward to offer her strength out of respect for *Odin*'s fallen son.

In all the attention to getting the ship corrected, *Nanna* saw her chance, and with a pace unable to be matched by those who had been distracted by the sand bumps along the way, she hurled herself into the inferno without so much as a scream. In fact, had those in attendance been able to have seen the moments before the fire took her, they would have seen what true contentment looks like for her heart was forever his, as was his in hers, so a life without the other was no life at all.

It almost seemed to the gods and mortals alike who were watching as though the fire was burning with a more steady, focused strength, as though the perfect fuel had been found; love, there is no substitute. Into the distance sailed the towering blaze, each flicker flames another spark of respect being paid to a beautiful being caught in something much too dark for the virtue of *Baldur*, and yet it is as it ended up occurring.

Frigg was finally feeling the weight of her part in this ordeal slip away, just like the burning ship over the horizon. Her thoughts lasted mere moments because, as she turned to see how her husband was handling the emotional tide of the ceremony, she saw that the horrible look in his eyes had only become stronger. She couldn't even begin to ask him what was on his mind when he turned to her and spoke.

"It's all going to happen," He paused, letting the whipping evening winds of the shoreline sting both their faces in the silence. *Frigg* felt every nanosecond of that pause and when he finally spoke again, she suddenly wished for that silence back,

"I've spent my strength, my time, and every bit of effort within me to somehow stave this off, but it's all going to happen just as I was shown. So long ago it has been now, and yet somehow not long enough—even when I knew somewhere in my mind that it would find me, I had hoped to be the victor and discover the way to outrun it. Though I suppose that is not how prophecy works, eh? Not really waiting on anyone or anything to validate it or make it feel better about itself; it's just *there*, right? Prophecies do little outside of waiting, I'd imagine, so this just waited for me to let my guard down and now all of this has—well, it's happened, hasn't it?"

Frigg couldn't find the words to break up his stream of thoughts that were spilling forth, and even though she was absolutely sure she knew what he was working up to, she was pleading with everything she could think of within herself that she was wrong and it was just the overwhelming nature of what he was going through. She knew she was wrong, and when *Odin* continued, his eyes still and colder than ever, he confirmed it.

"I had hoped that something would come and stop us from sending him off; some miracle that even the Fates didn't see coming. That didn't happen, as we can plainly see," He motioned into the distance where the dimming light of day was only bringing more focus to the still-burning pyre on the horizon,

"If it can't be stopped, and now with *Baldur* truly gone, that means I can't do anything about it. I had hoped with all this power—all the *Aesir* and the worlds and, well, just all of it, I had hoped it would be enough. It's still coming, though, *Frigg*, oh, my dear wife. It's all still going to happen…

"Ragnarök is coming."